ABOUT THIS BOOK

I0623510

He is tormented by the past. She is traumatized by her present.

Tied since birth to a darkness that longs to break free, spiritual psychic Harper Sinclair fights a never-ending battle with demonic spirits. Her only relief comes from the fallen angel whom she's long ignored deeper feelings for. Physically scarred and emotionally wounded from a year of fights and revelations, Harper is losing herself to the one thing she's always been afraid of: herself. And in the process, she's changing her relationship with the one friend she trusts the most.

Elias Jamison is a fallen angel. He lost his place in Heaven when he chose his friends over his creator. He fell, but he is not lost. For centuries, Elias maintained his innate goodness, fought against evil, and protected those in need—except for one. Grief-stricken, Elias pushed his loss aside for over one hundred years as he watched over the Freeman bloodline from afar, but the deeper his feelings grow for Harper Sinclair, the deeper old guilt digs in. Regret is a powerful tool when wielded against us, and vanquishing Harper's demons means confronting his own.

There's a little darkness in all of us. Are you ready to embrace it?

HAVENWOOD FALLS SIN & SILK BOOKS

Also try the signature line, Havenwood Falls, the historical paranormal line, Legends of Havenwood Falls, and stories from the local supernatural college in Sun & Moon Academy.

Stay up to date at www.HavenwoodFalls.com

ALSO BY R.K. RYALS

PARANORMAL ROMANCE BOOKS:

The Redemption Series

Redemption

Ransom

Retribution

Revelation

The Acropolis Series

The Acropolis

The Labyrinth

Deliverance

The Thorne Trilogy

Cursed

Possessed

Dancing with the Devil

In the Land of Tea and Ravens (Standalone book)

Havenwood Falls

Ink & Fire

Curse the Night

The Collector: Awakening

Dark Seduction

FANTASY BOOKS:

The Scribes of Medeisia Series

Mark of the Mage

Tempest

Fist of the Furor

City in Ruins

The Standalone Embrace Yourself Series

The Story of Awkward

An Introvert's Tale

CONTEMPORARY ROMANCE READS:

The Singing River

Hawthorne & Heathcliff

The Best I Could

Sex & Such

Capture the World

DARK SEDUCTION

A HAVENWOOD FALLS SIN & SILK NOVELLA

MICHELE G. MILLER

R.K. RYALS

To lovers of darkness

CHAPTER 1

HARPER

"Oscar Wilde," I whispered, the author's name rolling off my tongue, merely a breath in the middle of the night. The name was an odd thing to think aloud, but I'd been listening to an audiobook recently and, after the dream I'd just had, it was a Wilde quote I thought of as I locked gazes with myself in the mirror.

A dreamer is one who can only find his way by moonlight, and his punishment is that he sees the dawn before the rest of the world, I mouthed.

I thrived during the night, but I felt lost after the dawn. The darkness was my friend, the day my punishment for paying too much attention to the night. Hell, the darkness was my family, in the form of shadow demons and spirits. My constant companions.

My face was pale, my long brown hair a chaotic nest around my head, my eyes home to dark circles put there by too little sleep.

The bathroom mirror was too honest, telling me things I didn't want to know about myself.

As a spiritual writer who'd been brought into this world after my pregnant mother was stabbed by a necromancer's athame, I'd always been tied to darkness in one form or another. It was this gift that introduced me to the fallen angel who helped me understand myself and subsequently, the other fallen angel who became my closest friend.

It was Elias Jamison—my best friend—I thought of now, my gaze on my reflection. My breathing was too rapid, my heart pounding, beads of sweat clinging to my brow. All because I'd had a scorching hot, completely inappropriate dream about the man who'd slowly worked his way past my wall of defenses over the last year. I trusted him more than I did anyone else.

He'd helped save my life twice.

I wasn't an easy person to befriend. I was reclusive, but Elias didn't seem to mind. The way he checked in with me—the texts he often sent—was important to me. Which was why when he left recently, his absence affected me more than I thought it would.

Because you're angry, the spirits around me said bluntly.

"No," I argued. "It was good he left."

When Elias had disappeared on angel business, I honestly thought the distance would be good. I'd become too dependent on having him near. I needed to be more open with the friends I'd made recently, but while I'd become closer to the others in town the last year, especially after our recent alliance to battle against the one known as the Collector, it was still Elias I felt most comfortable with.

Until now. Until this dream. This was why I shouldn't sleep.

"Is this going to become a habit?" a snide voice asked. The bronze-barbed mace—he was basically a baseball bat on steroids—who lived with me bounced near the doorway, impatient and agitated. Desi—short for Destroyer—was a sentient weapon that shape-shifted into a huge lion with wings. He'd been a gift from the first and only lover I'd ever had. I didn't quite know what finally losing my virginity to a high-ranking fallen angel at twenty-three and being rewarded with a weapon said about me, but I was all about collecting odd experiences and memories.

Desi was annoying as hell, but I couldn't live without him. Some people spoiled their cats and dogs. I spoiled my ancient shape-shifting pet weapon. Go figure. He needed lots of love, attention, and validation.

"What woke you up this time?" Desi asked.

It wasn't a nightmare that had me this restless.

A red blush bloomed across my skin, and I turned on the sink to splash cold water on my face. Images of flesh on flesh, Elias's hands and lips in places I'd never imagined his hands and lips being before, burned into my subconscious. Elias was a big man, brawny and broad, a beard covering a handsomely rugged face. His voice was raspy, deep, and sexy in a rock star kind of way.

He'd called my name in the dream. Over and over again.

I stared at the running water, watching as it circled the drain and disappeared, the dream replaying in my head.

"Harper."

Elias breathed my name into my ear, surprising me, because I'd been asleep when he slid into bed behind me. His voice and the warm feel of his body woke me. I should have pushed him away, the shock of him being there bringing me to my senses, but all I felt was excitement and contentment.

"Finally," I whispered, *because I wanted this.* Really *wanted this.*

"Harper," he repeated, his arms pulling me into his embrace.

He was naked and hard. As was I—the naked part anyway—which was strange, because I didn't sleep naked. Tonight, however, there was only desire and need between us, his hand sweeping over the smooth contours of my stomach before slipping between my legs to caress me.

"You're wet," Elias said, satisfied.

His fingers slid through the moist heat to my clit, the sensation he caused with his touch so painfully pleasant that I almost lost it. My whimpers filled the room.

What was I doing? What were we doing?

"Elias—"

He stopped me with a kiss, rolling me over so quickly, I had no time to think before his lips crashed down onto mine, his tongue invading my mouth. His hand gripped my ass, our bodies pressed so closely together there was no space between us, the hard length of him hot against my belly.

"Tell me you're ready for me," he told me, pulling back to rest his forehead against mine, his breath fanning my lips.

"I'm ready."

He had me on my back in seconds, entering me quickly, as if he were afraid I'd change my mind. He filled me up completely.

"So tight," he growled.

His hips moved, and I lost the ability to think.

"Eli—"

I had woken on the verge of saying his name. My hand drifted to my stomach, the sudden tickle in my gut new and fresh and different.

"I want Elias," I heard myself say, my voice huskier and sexier than usual.

My eyes shot to the mirror, to the gaze staring back at me.

"What'd you say?" I asked myself. My free hand found my lips, my fingers tracing my mouth.

Desi snorted from his spot by the door. "Look what you've done to her. She's finally gone crazy," he said, his words directed at the dark spirits.

Shadow figures ducked in and out of the bathroom, ghostly images that played with my shower curtains and hissed at Desi.

Despite the chaos and their presence, the hand I had on my stomach drifted lower, and I jerked, forcing it up and away from my body.

"Out!" I yelled suddenly, my voice too rough. "All of you!" Embarrassment turned my skin hot, and I shooed the mace and ghostly shadows out the door before slamming it shut and turning to slide down to the floor. "Holy shit!"

I wasn't sure what bothered me more. The fact that I had been about to pleasure myself in front of a group of demonic spirits and a sentient weapon or the fact that I was about to masturbate while thinking about my best friend.

"What's going on with you, Harper?" I asked aloud.

The freaky thing wasn't me talking to myself or having sexy dreams about Elias. It's not like dreams could be controlled, and I talked to myself all the time.

It was the fact that I *answered* myself, my voice seductive when I said, "Being horny isn't bad. Not doing something about it is completely terrible for a person's health."

I knew what this was. This was me fighting with myself because part of me wanted what another part of me wasn't sure of, but fear and confusion shot down my spine nonetheless, immobilizing me. The last time I'd fought with myself like this, the last time I'd been this conflicted, was when I was taken captive by an evil doll—long story—and held in a creepy dollhouse for weeks in a nightmare that had ended with me physically wounded and emotionally bruised.

"No one understands you, Harper." The shadows returned, thick, dark, and seductive, their voices strong and powerful in my head. Their voices didn't sound like mine. I was used to their voices.

"But we *understand you. We understand you like no one else ever will. We understand your desire and your needs."*

Trembling, I slid back up the door and turned cautiously toward my mirror.

It was just me. The same plain Jane I'd always been—messy brown hair, scared green eyes, and a plaid pajama set that was two sizes too big.

This was the Harper I knew. Only there were dark forms crowded behind me, shadow people, their wispy, sinister arms outstretched as if to hug me.

"We are everything you will ever need and more."

Desi pounded on the bathroom door. "At least use the air freshener when you're done."

His light joke broke the tension, and the shadows scattered. A small, nervous laugh escaped me, my wide eyes dropping to my hands where they gripped the bathroom sink so tightly, the knuckles were white.

I felt like I was torn in two, completely divided between who I used to be and who I was tempted to be. I'd even started talking to myself in my sleep, getting up at night to leave written messages I found later. I'd once written a message in red lipstick on my mirror. It was hell to clean off.

Releasing the sink, I walked on unsteady, light feet from the bathroom, into the bedroom, and out into the kitchen. My hands were swifter than my brain, quick to make a cup of hot cocoa that I cradled in my palms, the warmth comforting.

Desi followed, quieter than he'd been before. It was hard reading him in weapon form. He didn't have eyes or lips. When he communicated, words were just *heard*. I didn't question how it worked. I was just glad he could speak, sarcasm and all, because he kept me from feeling lonely.

My mouth was full of hot chocolate when Desi murmured, "You feel different, and I don't think it's because you had a sex dream."

Holy hell!

Cocoa spewed everywhere. "You didn't just say that!"

"What did I say then?" he asked sweetly. "It's—"

"There are certain pet privileges you don't have."

"I'm not a pet," he spat.

Arguing was normal for Desi and me, but tonight it cloaked an entirely different problem. And it had nothing to do with dreams. I felt different. Antsy and impatient. As if my body was telling me I needed to *do* something.

My phone, which I rarely used because the signal tended to be bad in Havenwood Falls, lay on the kitchen counter, and I touched it lightly.

The urge to text Elias was strong, but I'd promised myself I wouldn't reach out to him until he returned. Elias had an entire life and problems of his own outside of me. Besides, it would be a little weird to text him after having an erotic dream about him, right? More so since it was the middle of the night.

I tapped the phone's screen and touched the messenger icon to scroll through our old texts. I was one of those people who never deleted anything.

Sweet memories surfaced, the messages a reminder of the first time I'd met Elias outside Coffee Haven. The day I realized he was open to befriending a naïve, shy girl who'd just experienced her first heartbreak and learned exactly how deep her ties to Hell and the spirit world went. Christmas in Havenwood Falls a year ago. Back when all I'd cared about was tackling a list of firsts.

A lot had happened in a year.

"You've got too much drama for being a loner. You need a fuck buddy." The moment the words left my mouth, my hands flew to my lips, my eyes widening.

Desi bounced up onto the counter, leaving scratches on the surface. He was going to ruin my house.

"Was that you?" he asked, incredulous.

It *was* me, but I was behaving differently than usual.

Me and *not* me.

"Because you have different needs now," the shadows revealed. *"Let go, Harper. Let go and be everything you were born to be. Listen to yourself."*

"Your eyes," Desi breathed.

Grabbing my phone, I clicked the camera icon and put it on selfie mode. My eyes were dilated, the black pupils completely overtaking the green.

"I'm pretty, aren't I?" I asked myself, a small smile lifting the corner of my lips.

Me and *not* me.

This me liked the way she looked in oversized plaid pajamas. She oozed a confidence about her messy hair and startled eyes that I lacked.

This me had a thing for fallen angel Elias Jamison, and she wasn't the kind to sit back and let him slide through her fingers.

"We know each other so well," I said aloud, my gaze on the camera. My finger pressed the picture key, my brows arched as it captured my image. "I should send this to him. I look good."

Was I possessed? All because of a sex dream? Did demons possess you if you had dreams about sex? Because if they did, the entire population was a walking exorcism project.

"Wow." Desi whistled. "You've officially lost your mind."

I didn't answer him because I was sending a picture text I wasn't sure I wanted to send.

CHAPTER 2

ELIAS

I flipped through my stack of mail and stomped up the stairs leading from the Ski-Ventures hangar to my residence, my boots bleeding slush and snow with each step, my hand stilling when I spotted familiar writing.

Miss us yet? Enjoy the snow!

Breckin and Viv. My smile was automatic. I flipped the postcard and was greeted by the cerulean water, golden sand, and lush foliage of the Maldives.

"Assholes."

Thanks to the Court, which had made a special exception to the rules on the memory wards that protected the town, the damn teens could traipse about the world without fear of forgetting home, while I was stuck in the frigid hell of Havenwood Falls, Colorado, in January.

But they're safe. That's what mattered.

I slapped my keys onto the hook by the door, then opened the drawer of the table sitting at the entrance to my place and dropped the postcard in with the rest. A postcard sent as they left each destination. Albania, Bhuton, Sri Lanka, now the Maldives. They hit destinations average eighteen-year-olds wouldn't consider, because unexpected meant harder to find.

Mentally exhausted from my own unexpected trip, I left the lights off and did a sweep of the place. I'd finished walking the rooms and was headed for the couch when my cell phone vibrated with an incoming call. *Hamon.*

Falling into the deep cushions, I answered the call on an exhale. "Yeah?"

"Everything secure?" Breckin's father asked with little emotion. He may have stepped away from leadership last spring, but Hamon would always be a commander.

"Everything's fine here. I stopped by the Medical Center and let Rachel know we were back."

"*You're* back," Hamon corrected. "I'm already on my way to Bintan."

"Bintan?" Bintan, an island in the South China Sea, was Hamon's base of operations when he played the role of dirty angel. After what happened with him, Breckin, and Viv down in Amartía—a playground, of sorts, for fallen and damned angels—I'd assumed he'd stay clean for a while. Apparently, I was mistaken.

"Do you think Andras and his crew were the only fallen after them, Elias? Did you think our trip to Latvia would be the last of its kind? While threats to Breckin and Vivienne remain, I can't walk away."

There would be more trouble, of course there would be. Hamon had amassed a long list of powerful enemies through the centuries. As a Nephilim, his son was a target. And Viv? Her bloodline and special connection with Breckin made her a larger target. That's the only reason the Court agreed to change the memory wards. Allowing Breckin and Viv to leave town, and still retain their memories, not only kept them safe from our enemies, but kept Havenwood Falls safe as well. No one wanted a bunch of fallen angels and demons with vendettas roaming this town. At least not the kind who had no qualms about shredding our peaceful community. I'd raised Breckin as my own, and I'd watched over Viv since birth, and her mother, Rachel, before her, and Rachel's mother before that. For more than a hundred years, I kept the Freeman women safe. All but one, and her loss had fueled Hamon's rebellion from the Divine—and my guilt—ever since.

9

"There are other ways. Ways that won't risk your redemption."

"Always worried about my redemption," Hamon said with a low laugh. "She would be proud."

"She'd call us idiots for all the shit we've done wrong through the years, that's what she'd do," I corrected as the dagger of her loss twisted. "Go to Bintan, gather intel, boss a few lowlifes around, then get your ass back here without inciting a war we don't need." I'd promised Breckin I would try my best to keep his father around.

"Take a break, Elias. Keep your eyes and ears open, maybe stay at the house with Rachel, but take a break. Give that cute little psychic of yours a call."

"She's a friend," I replied as evenly as possible. "And how in the hell would you know if she's cute?" All I needed was Hamon and his damn movie star face sniffing around Harper Sinclair.

Hamon chuckled. "Mm-hmm, sure she is. I'll keep in touch." He ended the call without giving me the opportunity to reply. Frustrated, I flipped my phone onto the coffee table.

Harper. Closing my eyes, I combed my fingers through my too-long beard as a vision of her face the last time I'd seen her played behind my eyelids. She was a mess after the ordeal with the Collector, her green eyes haunted, her brow permanently wrinkled, like her mind fought back a barrage of demons. She'd looked like hell, been through hell—and I'd left.

"You left her alone, like you left Phaedra alone," a voice skittered across my mind. My eyes snapped open. The living room was dark, but I could see everything clearly with my angel vision. There was no one here. I turned on the lamp anyway. A shadow seemed to move away as the feeling of something scraping against my brain shocked me. *"Alone and weakened,"* the voice teased.

"Fuck." Panic seized control. I jumped up from my couch and steered myself toward the bedroom, peeling off the filth-covered clothing I'd worn for days as I went. The shower door bounced off the wall as I flung it open and yanked on the hot water knob. While waiting for steam to appear, I grabbed fresh clothes, brushed my teeth, and laughed at the man reflected back at me over the sink. "It's fucking three in the morning. What's your plan here?"

"I'll drive by, make sure things are quiet. No big deal." I answered myself like a lunatic.

That's why you're taking a shower and putting on clean clothes? Because you're just driving by? My internal voice made a nuisance of itself.

Clearly, the man in the mirror believed my motives about as much as I believed in shaving. I glared at my reflection and turned toward the shower, in dire need of the hot water and a good head clearing.

While I lathered, shampooed, and rinsed, I shook my head at the crazy ride my thoughts took. Harper was fine. The fallen wouldn't hunt her as they had Phaedra. They couldn't connect me to her. We'd been friendly, social. There was no reason to worry. Not yet, anyway.

She was fine, but that didn't stop me from throwing on my clothes, grabbing the keys to my truck, and hauling my ass across town fifteen minutes later.

Just in case.

The first flakes fell before I hit Main Street. Fantastic. It was three in the morning, snowing, and I was driving to Harper's unannounced after weeks with no communication. *Checking things out, that's all*, I reminded myself.

Harper lived north of town in a secluded little mountain cabin she'd bought over a year ago. It was her first step toward finding herself after years of seclusion, thanks to her gifts. She loved the place. As her friend, and an overprotective one at that, I'd prefer it if she lived closer to town. Or other humans. Though the whispers that had toyed with my mind less than thirty minutes ago had not returned, the closer I came to Harper's, the tighter my grip on my steering wheel became.

Nerves maybe? I'd missed her more than I'd expected. Even after tracking four fallen ones across the Baltic states for weeks and ending them, the first thing I'd thought about when it was over was returning to Havenwood Falls and finally dealing with Harper and whatever was between us.

I frowned, bothered by my desire to see her, and slowed as the narrow drive to the cabin curved left, the path covered with thick snow. Hidden and untouched by tracks of any sort. By the looks of it, Harper hadn't left home in days.

As the trees thinned and the silhouette of her small cabin came into view, I cut my headlights and rolled to a stop on the edge of her property. The glow of the winter moon reflected off the white powder covering everything, giving me plenty of visibility along with my enhanced vision. I rolled down my window, then sat back and listened.

I stiffened and sniffed at the cold air, the vague scent of Hell making the hair on the back of my neck raise. Harper oozed darkness —it was sexy as hell—but tonight it was different. Stronger. I shoved back my angelic gifts as they rose to destroy the evil I sensed beyond her door. *She's not evil,* I reminded them. *Her darkness is beautiful. She's chosen goodness.*

And you think you can keep her that way, angel? The voice of doubt shouted in my ear.

My cell phone vibrated twice in the console, indicating a text. "So help me, if this is another picture of paradise from Breck . . ."

Harper, my screen read, with no message in the text field. I looked at the cabin, then back at my phone. Could she see me sitting out here, like the creeper I was? There was no message, but there was an attachment. My finger tapped the screen, almost reluctantly, as though it were afraid of what might pop up.

What greeted me was a picture so damn alluring, my jeans became uncomfortable. Her normally green eyes appeared nearly black as she stared at me with flirtatiously arched brows, a gently crooked smile, and the sexiest bedhead I'd seen in a long while.

I peered through the falling snow and searched for the telltale sign of her face peeking through a crack in the curtains. The rumbling of my truck must have woken her. I looked back at the phone again. *Shit.* There was something in that smile, something so not like the shy woman I'd come to know. I should have left, but I wasn't an idiot.

Elias: Can't sleep?

Harper: Not alone I can't. Not when I've been thinking about you. When are you coming back to town?

Not alone? Thinking about me? *Go home, Elias. This woman deserves better than a middle-of-the-night booty call.* And that's exactly what my body begged for. I typed a reply.

Elias: I walked through my door about an hour ago.

The three little dots that showed she was replying moved. Then stopped. Then moved again.

Harper: What are you doing?

My fingers touched the keys dangling from the ignition. *Go. The. Fuck. Home.*

Elias: I'm sitting outside your door.

CHAPTER 3

HARPER

*W*hat the hell was Elias Jamison doing outside my house?

"Yes!" I cried, triumphant, the flirtatious side of me happy to see he'd responded to the text while the rest of me revolted. I'd flirted with the man I considered my best friend, whether or not he considered me that in return.

I'd just changed the game. With a text. With words. It was always words that changed my life—first with a spiritual message from a demon a year ago, and now this.

I clutched my stomach, afraid to text back. Afraid to look outside my window. This new antsy feeling—not to mention the sudden lustful thoughts I was having—was not something I wanted to invite Elias into.

"I swear I'm not crazy!" I hissed.

"Is it you telling me that or this new psycho side of yourself?" Desi asked. He was enjoying this. "Life with you is never dull. Not recently."

I was not amused.

"And when did you start being rude to guests?" Desi asked, headed for the door. I knew exactly what he planned to do.

"Don't you dare!" I warned, horrified.

The door flew open, blowing in frigid air, the wind hitting me from across the room. A truck door slammed, and I pressed against my kitchen counter. Something about Elias, even with the trust I had in him, made me uncomfortable. In a good way.

The minute he stomped onto my porch, his burly frame filling my door, I knew I was in trouble.

"He'll bring nothing but misery," the shadows warned.

"Come in," Desi invited cheerfully.

Elias perused me, his sharp gaze searching my face. "Hey." His voice sent shivers down my spine. It always did. Even before the dream. He took a hesitant step into the room, his brows furrowing. "Feels like it's been longer than what it has."

My silence was loud, but I was scared to speak, scared of what might pop out of my mouth.

My front door closed behind Elias.

"Little late to be out, isn't it?" Desi asked the angel, amused. We were making his night.

Unlike with me, the mace never bothered Elias. Angels knew who and what the Destroyer was—an ancient weapon created by gods to fight alongside heroes and heroines. From the days when immortals walked the earth freely and legends were born until now, the mace existed to defeat and triumph.

"How have you been?" Elias asked me, ignoring Desi.

"G-good," I answered finally, tucking my messy hair behind my ears.

Elias's lips twitched, affection evident in his gaze, and for a moment I saw him the way I should see him. A good friend.

Until he moved.

Sauntering over to my kitchen counter, he propped his hip against it and leaned forward, bringing him a little too close despite the barrier between us. "Quite the text you sent, Harper?"

And there it was. The reason for our awkwardness.

He made it sound like a question, as if he was trying to figure me out.

I was trying to figure me out, too. Right along with why the hell my belly was a mess of fluttering butterflies.

"Quite the response I got," I replied, bolder than was usual for me.

"Response?"

"You showing up here."

Elias fidgeted. "I was checking in after being gone. I missed you."

Warmth and unease bloomed in my belly. Warmth because he'd been worried about me. Unease because his absence—because of the timing— was another reason for our awkwardness. I'd been healing from a physical and mental injury when he left.

"I'm okay," I whispered.

Elias's eyes narrowed. "Are you?" He leaned closer, his height enough to eliminate the space between us even with the counter. "The text, Harper."

He wasn't going to let that go.

I shrugged. "I was feeling photogenic."

"You are a terrible liar."

Truth was, I had no idea how to answer him.

"Maybe I wanted . . ." My words trailed off as Elias's eyes darted off to the side.

"They're still here," he said.

I knew he was talking about the shadows, the demons and dark spirits attracted to my kind of power.

"He hates us."

A sense of foreboding settled over me, my heart filling with dread. "They never left," I told him.

The shadows kept a healthy distance from Elias, their dark forms a smoky blackness against the walls near the bedroom.

Guilt flashed across Elias's face. He'd left right after our battle with the Collector, missing everything that had transpired since.

Time healed many wounds, but there hadn't been enough time for mine to scab over. Since my captivity, I'd been a mess of night terrors and prophetic dreams. My need for the shadows and their presence as well as their need for me had also grown.

Don't mock me! I told myself.

I wanted to hit my head against a wall.

"Have they bothered you?" Elias asked finally, his gaze tracking the shadow forms.

I could breathe around Elias in a way I couldn't breathe around anyone else. He calmed the darkness in me. Now, though, he was bringing out something just as terrifying.

"Lust," I answered myself aloud, the word a husky sigh I knew came from deep within me.

Elias turned back to me. "What?"

Desi laughed. "I should probably go away for a few days."

"Don't you dare!" Elias and I both commanded simultaneously.

It was obvious neither of us was comfortable with the way things were going between us at the moment. This was uncharted territory.

"They aren't bothering me," I replied, finally answering his question the way I'd meant to answer it, while backing farther into my kitchen. "As a matter of fact, I'm doing great."

My body was on fire, my cheeks heated, my hands wanting desperately to get rid of my clothes and his.

"You s-should really go." My words came out ruder than I meant them to. "*Be angry at him!*" the shadows yelled within my mind.

Elias rounded the counter.

I grabbed at a kitchen towel hanging from the handle of my oven to hold it up like a shield. "Don't."

"What's up with you, Harper?" he asked, genuinely concerned.

If he came any closer, I was going to do something I wasn't sure I'd regret, but I wasn't sure he'd be open to.

"You know, I'm actually not feeling all that well. Could be contagious. Maybe—"

"I don't get sick."

"Elias," I whispered.

He leaned down, and I did the one thing I knew would change our relationship forever. For better or for worse.

CHAPTER 4

ELIAS

*H*arper's tongue shoved its way into my mouth with the aggression of a sex-starved teenager, and I shifted back, off balance at the unexpectedness of her move. The small step drew our lips apart just enough that Harper gasped and looked up, her eyes clouded with confusion. Her pupils were completely dilated, the shadows infiltrating her home coming closer.

"You stopped. Why did you stop?" Her face collapsed, her small fists suddenly pounding my chest. "You're not supposed to stop."

Her words were thick with desire, but there was also anger.

"Whoa." More worried for her safety than mine, I caught one of Harper's wrists and twisted, pinning her arm to her side. "What the hell, Harper?"

Her shadows pushed closer still—crowding around her feet and spitting obscenities. Their hatred for me—an intruder—was evident in every vile comment they hissed my way.

"Make me forget," she begged, her eyes welling with tears. "Why won't you make me forget? You owe me that much."

Fuck. Me. My hand shoved into the mass of hair at her nape.

"Owe you for what?" I asked, my gaze holding hers.

Harper's emotions were at war. Desire curved her body invitingly into mine even as torment clouded her eyes. Why bother asking? I'd left when she'd needed me. I was an asshole. And this confusing woman—who was both light and dark, powerful in ways I wasn't sure she yet knew—had me tangled up in emotions I couldn't process. I knew sex. I knew pleasure. But this? This was something entirely different.

This was Harper. She was unlike any woman I'd ever met.

"Elias?" My name was a petition whispered in the breath between us.

I licked at my bottom lip, and Harper lifted on her toes with a whimper. Fueled by guilt, and a good dose of lust, my right hand slid over her ass and gripped the curve of her thigh. "I didn't drive over here to seduce you."

She stiffened, desire becoming rage, before pushing at me. "Why not seduce me? Seduction is better than abandonment." She laughed coldly. "It seems I'm much better at being seduced than making people stay."

Lucas. Damn him! I ached at Harper's vulnerability. It radiated from her being the way Lucas's mark colored her aura. It was that mark, that iridescent blue hue of another fallen angel, that made me keep my distance, romantically, for more than a year. Lucas didn't own her. He never claimed he did. But loyalty to a long-ago comrade had tied my hands. I'd thought he might return to her. I should have known better. Very few angels settled down. We were warriors, protectors, the ones with Divine knowledge of what had been and what will come—we weren't created to play house with humans. We were merely biding our time, and choosing sides, until the end.

Lucas had hurt her more than I'd realized. I was happy she'd allowed herself to be angry, but . . .

I leaned against the counter and crossed my arms. "Who is talking to me right now, Harper? I'll take the anger if that's what makes *you* feel better, but I'll be damned if I let those little shits—"

"Are you attacking them, Elias?" She waved her hands at the room, at the spitting shadows flanking us. "They've been there for me."

Fury filled my chest like a child's balloon as I glared at our audience. "Oh, to hell with that. *I'm* here for you," I countered, my fingers snagging her oversized top to tug her against my chest. "I won't abandon you. I'm not him, Harper."

She pushed at me again, ducking out of my embrace to move away from me. Her fist hit the countertop and dishes rattled in the cabinets below. The sound seemed to set her off, and she spun. Jerking open another cabinet above her head, she grabbed a glass tumbler and threw it. It flew across the room to shatter against her wall.

I started, shock momentarily paralyzing me. No matter what emotions Harper was feeling, this wasn't entirely Harper.

Yanking her toward me, I gripped her chin. "Do you want my kisses?" I ground out, my fingers digging into her skin. Harper fought my grip. I won.

Grinning at her submission, as minuscule as it was, I dropped my forehead to hers and slipped my free hand beneath her top. "You want me to touch you, Harper?" Twin flashes of red colored her cheeks when my fingertips brushed the underside of her bare breast. She leaned into my touch, her desire evident in her scent, her coloring, the way her throat moved as she swallowed. Her eyes said yes, when her voice didn't. Anger hardened my features. "Then get rid of the damn shadows."

We held our positions, deadlocked in this battle. Then her defiance disappeared. I tensed at the change.

"You want us gone?" she asked, smiling sweetly. "Are you that afraid of the darkness, angel?"

Rage blinded me at her use of *us*, sending my arms around her waist and back, as I kicked Harper's leg and swept her off her feet. We hit the wooden floor and Harper growled and bucked, her hands pushing at my shoulders while I straddled her hips.

"Get the fuck out," I said through a growl of my own, my hands catching hers and pinning them over her head. "You do not control her."

I released the damper on my powers, sending a flood of light across the kitchen.

"You can't have her," I said as I dropped my elbows on either side of her face. My hands still gripped her wrists above her head. The shadows screeched as my power hit them in pulsing waves. My eyes studied hers, watching for their change. "She's mine." The truth of the sentiment burned my throat like a brand.

On a heavy exhale, Harper went from fighting me to lying still, her dilated pupils returning to normal. "Elias . . ." Her words trailed off, guilt leeching the color from her face. She inhaled, as if bracing herself. "I-I . . ."

I maintained my position—my hands locked around her wrists, my body hovering over hers. I should have released her, but I couldn't. I didn't want to. "How often have they done that since I left?"

"Often enough." It was obvious by her pained expression that Harper may have been consumed by shadows, but she'd been coherent the entire time. "I want to tell you I'm sorry, but I can't. I won't." Tears leaked from her eyes.

I bent lower, bringing our chests flush, and released her arms. My hands went straight to her jaw, cupping it. "Don't." I swiped at her damp cheeks. "You don't owe me, or anyone else, apologies, Harper. You're allowed to be angry. Though I'd prefer for you to tap into those emotions without the help of your little friends. Think we can work on that?"

She hesitated. "What if part of me doesn't want to do it without them?"

"I'll be here to help, regardless." I kissed her forehead and moved to stand over her. "But I know you have the strength to do it on your own." I offered her my hand.

Harper stared at my palm. "I'm not sure you know what you're getting yourself into." Her fingers slipped into mine. "I-I think I prefer forgetting," she stuttered, almost shyly, as I brought her to her feet.

"Forgetting, huh?" I asked with a wink and, once again, my hand found its way around the curve of her ass. "I could help with that. If you want me to?" I drew her leg up toward my waist.

Her unease cleared at my question, her earlier brazen confidence returning with it.

"Are you finally seducing me, Elias Jamison?" she asked as she walked her fingers up my chest until she cupped my neck. We'd crossed a line tonight, and neither one of us wanted to go back.

"If I were seducing you, Harper Sinclair, I'd be buried between your legs and you'd be screaming my name already."

Her fingernails sank into my skin. "Show me."

My mouth collided with hers, my tongue sweeping from one side to the other, with as much grace as a drunk sailor after nine months at sea. Harper moaned, then bit my tongue gently. Before she released her bite, I had her propped on the edge of her countertop, both legs wrapped firmly around my backside, my fingers unbuttoning her plaid pajama top.

I'd liberated three buttons when a muttered "It's about time" came from somewhere in the cabin. *Desi.*

Harper wrenched back with a gasp, and my gut tightened. I stole a glimpse of the flesh beneath her top before my hands went to her knees to unwrap myself from her legs. Leaving my palms resting gently on the tops of her thighs, I stared down at her flushed face and perplexed expression.

My knuckles brushed over Harper's beard-rashed chin. "He's a pain in the ass, isn't he?"

"It's not my fault you two turned me into a voyeur," Desi said from wherever he hid. "I offered to go."

He poked out from around the bottom cabinet, and I pinned him with a glare. "You're not allowed to leave her side, *Destroyer.*"

My hands settled on Harper's hips, and I picked her up and lowered her to the floor as Desi snorted. "I never pegged you for an exhibitionist, angel."

Harper leaned her shoulder into my chest as she turned toward the mouthy mace, a comical look of exasperation on her tired face. "Go away."

For a weapon with no actual facial features, he came off as rather disgruntled when he huffed and bounced out of the kitchen. "Tell me to stay, tell me to go," he mumbled as he passed by my foot.

"Go cuddle one of Harper's pillows, if you're lacking companionship."

Laughing softly from my arms, Harper poked my side. "You're antagonizing him."

"I'm sure he'll return the favor."

"You know I will," Desi shouted before a door slammed shut.

I lifted a brow and caught Harper's gaze. Her hands clasped in front of her chest as we parted awkwardly. Now that the ardor had cooled, and Desi had left, our aborted kiss hung between us.

I covered her wringing hands with mine. "Let's get you to bed. You have to be exhausted."

"Stay with me?"

At Harper's urging I lay—fully clothed (my requirement; I knew my limits)—on my back as she snuggled into my side, her face resting in the dip between my arm and chest. She fell asleep quickly, her arm heavy across my waist. I spent the hours counting her breaths and watching the way her shadows lingered in her bedroom. They kept their distance, a very good thing for them, because I was in the mood to kick some demon ass for what they'd done to her.

She'd come to rely on them while I was away. I should have considered that possibility before I'd left. I would not let the darkness consume her. I would show Harper how to live life. A life she controlled.

CHAPTER 5

ELIAS

*H*arper rushed out her door as I pulled up in front of her cabin just after noon the next day, a smile on her face. She waved for me to stay in the truck as she locked up, and I took the moment to appreciate the view. Her tiny frame was bundled up against the cold in layers of clothing. She looked like a colorful snow woman. *A hell of a sexy snow woman*, I thought when she turned my way, her ever-present backpack, also known as Desi's ride, swinging from her hand as she crossed the yard, then climbed into my truck.

She looked more Harper-like today. It wasn't fair of me to assess her that way, but it was true. Her demon shadows lingered in the cab and around the truck as we drove, gently sweeping her shoulders when they got the chance, as if caressing her. But her eyes were a twinkling bright green—happy, excited—which meant she was keeping them at bay. I reached across the cab and snagged the thick braid pulled to the side of her head beneath her red knit hat. "Thank you for coming today."

Harper's lips pursed as I tugged her hair. "Thank you for asking me out."

I'd woken her early this morning, telling her I needed to run some errands before asking her to join me for the day at the town's annual Winterfest celebration—our first official date. A badly needed date, after a year of tiptoeing around our feelings, my weeks away, and last night's battle. She'd eagerly agreed.

We parked two streets over from the square, and I rounded the back of my truck to grab the large duffel I'd packed earlier as Harper jumped down from the passenger side. Her brows lifted when she caught sight of the heavy bag on my shoulder.

"So I did something." I held out my hand and her gloved fingers slipped around mine. A shadow hissed at my side, then disappeared.

"You did something?" Harper prompted. We moved with the rest of the pedestrian traffic and walked toward the square. "Do I want to know what you're carrying in that bag?"

"I figured it was time I got to see just how talented you are with those hands of yours." My words caused Harper to stumble, her mouth parting slightly as she looked up at me. I grinned wickedly. "With art, my little *umbra amans*. Your mind is terribly dirty these days."

Harper inhaled sharply, her shadows nearing at my words. It was an endearment, *umbra amans*—shadow lover. They circled Harper like lovers, constantly weaving inky paths in her presence. And the way she embraced them . . .

"You play with fire, angel," hissed the little guilt demon who'd suddenly appeared at my side. Walking on, I pretended he didn't exist. If Harper heard the shadow's comment, she ignored it as well. She threw me a thoughtful side-eye through her dark lashes as we entered the square, and I steered her toward a table with sign-in sheets.

Nodding to the teen volunteer, I took a plastic numbered snowflake stake and turned to Harper. "In case you hadn't guessed, I signed us up for the snow sculpture contest."

Winterfest was a celebration of all things ice and snow. Like every Havenwood Falls festival, this one had food, live performances, and booths selling themed items, but the main attractions were the competitions: one for ice castles, the other for snow sculptures. The residents in this town came out of the woodwork for competitions, even on below-freezing days. When it came down to it, Havenwood Falls was a bunch of supernatural beings trying to prove whose species was best in the only way the Court would allow—random contests. There were plenty of humans here, too. Competitiveness wasn't owned by the supes. Hell, the humans carried feuds as spitefully as the shifters and vamps did.

"Does it bother you?" Harper asked suddenly.

Stepping out of the line forming at the table, I closed the gap between us. "Does what bother me?"

"You called me a shadow lover. I—"

"*My* shadow lover," I corrected, my arm slipping between Harper and Desi's backpack to draw her closer. "I called you my shadow lover. There are things that bother me about you, Harper Sinclair, but that is not one of them." What her shadows intended for her bothered me. What bothered me even more were the emotions she brought out in me. Breckin was right—love was such a human sentiment. A feeling angels shouldn't have. But this human had sparked the forbidden inside of me.

Her concerned gaze searched the area. She didn't like drawing attention.

I cleared my throat. "Hey, don't worry about everyone else. Look at me."

Darkened green eyes found mine. They weren't completely dark; she was still there. "They hate you."

I spied one of her shadows ducking toward me. My face lowered, my lips brushing hers. "They can kiss my ass."

I gave her no chance to reply or address the public kiss I'd just given her in front of half the town. Instead, I applied pressure to her back, leading her toward the other end of the town square.

When we found our assigned spot—number nine—I dropped my bag of tools at the base of a mound of snow shoveled in by the event organizers for each contestant and circled the area.

Scratching at my beard, I cursed myself. How in the hell did I end up here?

A shriek followed by a masculine peal of laughter drew my attention over my shoulder in time to see Graysin Ravenal shove Weston Everett into their mound of half-sculpted snow.

"This is a family event, Everett!" She kicked at the pile. "I can't take you anywhere." Behind them, Callie Montgomery and Ronan Bishop stood watching as Graysin's tantrum continued, "I can't believe I was sitting here stroking the shaft, trying to get it nice and smooth . . ."

"Stroking it, huh?" Everett chuckled from the snow bank. Graysin dropped her head with a self-deprecating groan and slapped at his leg.

Ronan snickered at whatever Weston had sculpted, and Callie pinched his side, as her whispered "Don't you dare laugh" carried my way.

"For once, I can't fault the guy. I'd have revolted, too, if you'd forced me into that."

Callie fought back her own laughter. "You would have formed a massive hard-on?"

Leaning into her side, his cool blue eyes held hers. An intimate look passed between them, and I averted my gaze, but I couldn't help but catch his words. "I always form massive hard-ons when I'm with you."

I snorted, and Ronan's attention jerked my way. My hands rose in apology for eavesdropping. It's not like I could help my angelic hearing.

Ronan nodded. "The shit we do for our women, huh?"

Glancing up, Callie's face turned bright red when she caught my stare, before her gaze landed on Harper behind me. Or so I assumed, from the curious grin forming on her lips as she moved to help Graysin.

I turned to Harper, ready to tease her about Ronan's comments, but she wasn't there. I looked over the snow mound to find her outside our little roped-off work area, hugging herself, her hands rubbing at her arms as she glanced about the festival. Her shadows gathered around her, as if they wanted to keep her warm but she wasn't letting them. It was odd seeing dark spirits acting chivalrous. Most of them lingered at her feet and legs, like stray cats seeking attention, but one loitered near her shoulders, floating from one ear to the other.

"You don't belong with him, Harper," it whispered. *"This will only hurt you in the end, not him."*

The little bastard.

"Harper?" I scooped a handful of snow from our pile and walked toward her carefully, like one would approach a frightened child, my actions agitating the shadows. "Stepping out, remember? Remember that first-time-for-everything list you were so adamant about a year ago?"

Harper blinked once, then twice, her nearly black eyes coming into focus as I drew closer. There was something so exposed about Harper since her abduction and captivity last month.

"I thought we could sculpt Desi in his winged lion form," I suggested, reaching for her. All but the shadow at her shoulder slinked away.

Her backpack shook. "I like that idea," the mace with the giant ego sang.

Harper looked at me, her wrinkled brow smoothing. I kept speaking. "Though I thought we could improve on him some. Maybe give him a hump?"

Desi hissed. "I am a lion with majestic wings the likes of which you've never had, angel."

He had me there. "A horn, then? Desi, the uni-lion?"

A strangled laugh burst from Harper's mouth. "You're egging him on," she managed as Desi grumbled. The black slowly leaked from her eyes.

"I am," I admitted, drawing her into our work space. "But only to get a smile out of you. You okay?"

She nodded. "Sorry. I don't think I've gotten over it . . . everything that happened with the Collector. I feel . . . exposed somehow, being out here."

I released the damper on my power, allowing my energy to scare her demons away. After last night, I'd withdrawn the force I used over them, out of respect for her relationship with the darkness. But seeing her like this shattered my willingness to allow them to siphon away her strength. The last shadow hissed and floated back.

I tilted her chin and cupped her face. "Harper, nothing is going to hurt you here. Look around."

Her eyes danced around the square to study the people enjoying this sunny, but cold, Saturday in January.

"Whatever you're worried about isn't going to happen on a day like today. And, if it did, I'm here." I drew her gaze back to mine. "Desi and I won't let anything hurt you again."

It wasn't my fault she'd been hurt. I wasn't in her life then, or not in any way that counted. I wasn't officially in her life now either, but that was fast changing. As complicated as things would be between us —a semi-fallen angel and a psychic tied to demons—I wanted it to happen.

Harper lifted to her toes and kissed the side of my mouth, her hand on my shoulder for balance. "A winged lion with a horn?" she asked playfully. "I like it."

We spent the next several hours carving a winged Desi, sans horn, out of snow. Harper's hands were artistically talented, as I knew they would be. She was drawn to art and photography, and had a good eye.

I admired the wings she'd built up, her hands deftly wielding the metal tools I'd brought to individually carve out each feather. "It's a shame you weren't able to draw growing up."

Biting her lip, she leaned back and studied her work. "I wanted to, but when all you see is death and fear every time you touch pen or paper, you lose interest. A beautiful hobby becomes a very scary undertaking."

"Hey, Harper," a high school guy who'd worked with his friends and flirted with Harper all afternoon from our left side suddenly called, his eyes full of hope. "We're going to get some hot cider. Would you like some?"

Harper threw me an embarrassed glance. "Um, I'm good, but thank you for offering."

The teen's face fell, but he nodded and turned back to his smiling friends. The boys were amused by their buddy's rejection. His *no big deal* face reminded me of Breckin's during his teenage years when he'd been let down. Feeling embarrassingly parental, I jumped to my feet under the pretense of needing to examine our work from another vantage point.

As Harper lowered her head and went back to making wings, I stopped the guy. "She's too old for you and spoken for, but if you buy her a hot chocolate, she'll think you're a hero."

Handing him five bucks, I watched him and his buddies take off, pushing and shoving each other as they went.

The clock on the competition ticked toward the finish time— thirty minutes. I knelt by Harper's side, my knuckles brushing the joint Harper had expertly carved in Desi's wings. "If I didn't know any better, I would think you had wings of your own."

"Why is that?" she asked while using her fingernail to fuss with a curved line she'd created in a feather. Her fingertips were bright red.

When did she take off her gloves?

Sighing, I took her hands in mine. They were icicles. "Because you've formed those like someone who has studied wings. It wouldn't be hard to believe they were real. The details . . ." I trailed off as I drew her fingers to my lips and blew on them.

Harper leaned in. "What were yours like?"

I felt, rather than saw, the return of her shadows as I considered her question. Their chittering laughter was louder than usual, mocking me and the painful loss of my wings.

Demons danced around us, and Everett Weston's frame came into view over Desi's ice wings, his brows furrowed in silent question. Most of the supes in Havenwood Falls wouldn't sense or notice the shadows, but as a gargoyle, Everett did. As much as I'd love to watch the gargoyle dropkick the sons of a bitches into next week, I cocked my head back, letting him know things were fine. Harper needed to figure out her shadow demons on her own without my interference.

My silence hung between us.

Harper attempted to tug her hands free from mine. "You don't have to talk about it if you're not comfortable discussing it."

"No." I tugged back, maintaining my hold, before I lowered our intertwined hands between us. "You can ask me anything, Harper. The only way this works is if we're willing to discuss the ugly stuff along with the good."

Her reply was cut off by her high school suitor's reappearance, a large cup of steaming liquid cradled in his hands.

"Um, I know you said you didn't need anything, but I brought you some hot chocolate." He circled our Desi sculpture, remaining far enough away to ensure Harper would have to leave my side if she wanted the drink.

She stood, her awed thank you filling the air as she hugged the boy. Her icicle-cold fingers eagerly wrapped around the cup, a sigh escaping as she took her first sip. "Oh, you're my hero!"

"I figured you could use the warmth considering all the work you did." His brown eyes flicked from Harper's euphoric face to mine. I gained my feet. "This lion is awesome, by the way."

His friends chimed their agreement. I had to concur that we made a good team. Our Desi looked just like the real one.

I glanced at the backpack the mace had spent the day hidden away in. What would he think of our project?

"Thanks, you guys did great, too. I like your . . . um, car?" Harper said.

Stepping behind her, I placed a hand on her waist. "That's not a car, Harper. That's an Audi R8."

The teenagers nodded appreciatively just as the bell signaling the end of the competition blared through the square.

"There's a difference?" Harper whispered.

"Between a car and an Audi? Yeah."

Releasing a little harrumph, Harper took a long sip of her drink before bumping her hip into my side. "By the way, don't think I didn't notice the little collar and tag you carved around his neck."

Grinning, I looked at my handiwork hanging from snow Desi's neck. "You do treat him like a pet."

By the time we'd cleaned up our tools and the judging had concluded —we came in second to a group of girls who'd sculpted mice in a winter scene I didn't bother checking out—the sun was gone and the square was aglow with lights.

"A lion losing to mice." I chuckled, speaking loud enough for Desi to hear. "Must be demoralizing."

Harper's backpack shook. I swiped the bag from the ground and threw it over my shoulder. "Just messing with you, Des. We absolutely should have won."

With Harper's agreement, we wandered through the booths. While we ate and browsed, I told her about my wings. "They were black, an inky black, like a fresh oil slick—you know the way the colors shimmer upon the oil? A sheen of blues and greens?" She nodded. "Dominion wings are quite large, rising above our heads and draping to the ground when resting. They were a symbol of pride, as they are for all angels."

"And you lost them in a battle."

"Yes. I was ambushed. I would have run and avoided the fight, but they used Phaedra to draw me in. By the time I realized I was too late to save her, it was too late to save myself, too."

She didn't bother telling me she was sorry for my loss, and I was glad. Instead, she weaved her arm through mine, touching her head to my shoulder as we walked.

"This public display of affection is bound to have the coffee shop talking in the morning."

Harper laughed. "I'll have to call Aunt Eloise, and tell her about our date right away, then. She'll be ecstatic. She thinks I'm a prude, but then this *is* the same woman who decided to reclaim her virginity in her forties just because she thought it would make the experience feel new . . ."

I chuckled at her eccentric aunt. There was likely no need for Harper to call her. The way this town worked, her aunt already knew we'd spent the day together.

We had conquered a Havenwood Falls town event together. She looked content and unguarded, and it made me smile to see her that way.

"Okay, Harper Sinclair, you've won second place in the ice sculpture competition, stuffed your face with traditional festival food, and gone on a date with a hot angel. What's next on your list of firsts?"

I asked as we headed back to my truck. It was almost eleven o'clock, and we'd shut down the festival before moving to the bookstore to find a quiet corner to enjoy more hot chocolate and chat.

Harper chuckled. "Is that what today was? You trying to help me check off my bucket list of things I've never had the courage to do?"

I lifted a shoulder. "It was about finding out if we were as compatible as I thought we were, despite our differences."

Snatching her hand, I pushed her against a building and lowered my mouth to her jaw. I licked at her skin. Her shadows whined. *Screw them.*

CHAPTER 6

HARPER

*M*y eyelids fluttered closed as Elias's lips found mine. We'd held hands, he'd hugged me, but his lips hadn't touched mine today, until this moment. I sank into his embrace. Savored his taste.

Elias groaned, my name falling from his lips in a low, gravelly tone.

The memory of him calling out to me as he plunged into my body hit me. My dream . . .

Lust ignited within as Elias pressed me against the wall, jagged bricks digging into my shoulders. The pain felt good.

"Elias," I said, the word strangled against his lips. He pulled back. Tears choked the back of my throat, and I coughed them away.

"Harper?" he asked gently.

"Find relief, Harper. What you want isn't something the angel can give. We can help you find it."

Their promises stirred my restlessness. Yes, I needed relief. Their dark laughter caressed my ear, and my body jerked, like it wanted to move toward them.

No! My gaze slid up to Elias's face. I wanted him. I wanted to let go and be with someone else, skin to skin and breath to breath. I wanted to share everything I felt, both good and bad, with someone.

The shadows understood that. They just didn't approve of the person I was with now.

"Do you want to go back to your place?" Elias asked.

Just do it, Harper, I told myself. I'd prepared myself for this moment. Hoped for it, even.

His eyes narrowed when I didn't respond right away. "This isn't about sex, Harper. I want more from you."

Shadowy fingers stroked me, the spirits' whispers urgent and needy in my head. *"Sex is a good thing. He makes it sound like a sin. Show the angel who you are."*

My body itched, my skin crawling with desire and power. I knew this feeling. I cleared my throat. "I have an idea."

Elias smiled, curiosity burning in his gaze. "I don't know whether to be excited or wary of the look in your eyes."

"Be both," I replied. "You should definitely be both."

Tonight I was going to do the least Harper thing I'd ever done, and I wasn't going to feel bad or guilty about it.

Offering Elias my hand, I wrapped my fingers around his and tugged him toward his truck. "Let's go."

Elias was quiet when I directed him back to my place and told him to use his angelic magic to change his clothes, while I hurried to my bedroom and changed my own. He was even quieter when I stepped out of my bedroom in a skintight black shirt and miniskirt with heels. However, he did visually devour me from head to toe before he used his angel gifts to match my attire with his own—snug black slacks and an obscenely fitted dress shirt that molded to his muscular torso so completely my panties were damp before we left my cabin.

Though his eyes flicked to my face throughout the drive that followed, he remained quiet as we drove back through town, past darkened houses, and finally to a secluded parking lot down a hidden road off County Road 13.

Located in a network of caves accessible only by a gondola lift, the establishment I took Elias to now was not publicly acknowledged by many people in Havenwood Falls, though most, if not all, residents of age knew it existed.

My pulse accelerated as I stared out the windshield at the gondola lifts before I climbed out of the truck, took a deep breath, and rubbed my gloved hands together.

Surprise marred Elias's features when he slid out of the vehicle, but he still didn't speak. It was as if he was afraid of breaking the spell I'd created by coming here at all. Even my shadows were subdued, hanging back in a pack as though they were watching and waiting for what came next.

Hand in hand, we walked toward the bouncers who checked IDs just outside the lift. I stole a glance at the angel beside me, curious about his thoughts, as he nodded solemnly at the men, then placed his hand on my hip. His eyes remained straight ahead, but the edge of his mouth twitched as we stepped into one of the gondolas and started up the side of Miles Mountain. A nameless emotion built in my gut the higher we went. Elias rubbed my back.

Once we paid the high cover charge and entered the establishment, Elias finally found his voice. "Somehow this was not what I was expecting from you."

I laughed. "Remember that list of firsts?"

"I remember that girl who listed 'making friends' as one of her firsts." He shook his head, a smirk on his lips. "I think she matured."

A shadow brushed past my calf, and I shivered as the look in Elias's eyes turned me bolder. "Maybe I have a different kind of list now."

Elias's hand crept up and gently gripped the back of my neck as he lowered his lips to the shell of my ear, his breath hot. "Well then, show me what you've got."

"Dance with me." Music pulsated throughout the entire room, the beat a sultry *thump, thump* that felt like an external heartbeat. My body reveled in it, my hips swaying along with the other patrons in the cavern. My clothes felt too hot against my skin, my hands pulling at the fabric to fan myself.

This was lust, one of the many emotions I'd cut myself off from.

One of the many sensations I wanted to explore without worrying about regrets.

Silk was just the place for that.

An upscale nightclub in Havenwood Falls, Silk was an establishment where the very rich and those specially invited could fulfill their fantasies or get their kink on, all in a safe environment closely monitored and controlled by the female hellhound who owned it, Melaina Savage.

The main area had bars, tables with stools, lounge areas, a VIP area, and a dance floor. Off the main room was a secure area that was a little edgier for supes only, a place where they could drop all pretenses and be themselves while partaking in exotic drinks and exotic fun.

After my recent involvement with the Court, and the new additional powers I'd discovered, I'd earned my right to the club and the supes area. The shadows tailing me were as excited as I was the farther we moved into the club, their dark forms weaving in and out of the patrons' undulating bodies. Something about the way the spirits glided along the skin, causing those who couldn't see them to shiver from a sudden chill, turned me on.

Reaching back, I grabbed Elias by the hand, my eyes wide and bright when I glanced up into his face. "Can you feel it?"

Energy. This place was bursting with energy. As if, at any moment, the building would explode. It hummed through me, followed by a barrage of voices in my head, and I found myself laughing—a joyful, wicked sound that poured out of me.

"There are so many of them here," I gasped. The shadows were everywhere, the usual group of spirits that followed me having doubled. They were always there in the darkness, waiting, the need in me having called them forth from Hell.

Elias pulled me close, the hand he had on me possessive, his gaze focused on the room.

"So many people," I breathed. "And spirits."

I'd never felt so close to life and death simultaneously. Psychics bridged a gap between the living and the dead, but most of the time there was a firm line between the two. Even if a psychic was strong enough to see the dead, he lived in the world of the living and merely *channeled* the beyond. Lately, I felt like I *lived* in both worlds, with one foot out of the grave and one foot in it. It was an odd sensation that made me feel like the rope in a game of tug of war, but it wasn't a terrible feeling. It was exhilarating.

"Harper?" Elias called. I'd pulled away from him, my body making its way through the throngs of people until I was at the edge of the room, near the stage.

My body was on fire, the lust building up in me ready to explode. This was part of who I was now. Demons fed off greed, lust, power, and gluttony. Amongst other things. And I was feeding off it, too. Partly because of the shadows' influence. It wasn't sex and lust the shadows had a problem with. Because of the shadows, and the power I was gaining from them, I wanted to do naughty things I wouldn't have dared before. It was the power that made me antsy, the power that had turned me into this new impatient and seductive person. I needed to quit ignoring it.

"Feed the need, Harper. There are men here who want you. Can't you feel that?" The shadows pressed up against me. *"Pick one. Any of them. Except the angel."*

"Harper," Elias called again.

I was lost to sensation, want, and need. I felt like I was free-falling, as if I'd bungee jumped from a cliff, cushioned by air and adrenaline. By power.

A hand wrapped around my upper arm. "Harper," Elias breathed.

There was a low whistle, the sound sultry and pleased. "Well, this is new. I've had necromancers in my club and never felt the presence of the dead like I do today." Melaina Savage appeared through the crowd, her dark hair swept up, the style accentuating the plunging neckline of her tight dress. Her stiletto heels drew the eyes to drool-worthy legs, but it was the satisfied look on her face that garnered the most attention.

"And not just any kind of dead," she continued, her gaze flicking to the shadows hovering near us. "Hello, Harper." Her eyes shone, a pair of special contacts keeping her stare from being deadly. If a human looked into a hellhound's eyes three times, he would die. Some supernaturals were immune to the glare—Elias for example—but even with my tie to the Infernum, I wasn't sure if I was.

"Melaina," I greeted her, my voice shaky but confident. My shadows spoke for me and with me. Tonight, we were one.

She winked, her breath pushing against my ear when she whispered, "Your shadows are hungry, darling. They're good for my business, the lusty need you are drawing off of each other being fed to the crowd. But if you lose control of them . . ." Her warning trailed off, a sudden red glint sparkling in her eyes.

Spirits often influenced the living without the living even being aware of it. A cold spot in a room. A sudden angry outburst by a normally calm person. A sudden sense of sadness when there was no reason to be sad.

My spirits and I were bleeding lust.

"You don't need to worry," Elias said fiercely, his broad frame dwarfing my thinner, smaller one.

"Don't I?" Melaina asked, arching her brows at the angel. "They say it's the quiet ones."

I giggled, and then rushed to cover my mouth. My head was spinning. Shadows danced close and then edged away, keeping a healthy distance from the angel at my side. The hellhound, they approached, but didn't mess with.

Melaina shook her head. "For that kind of power, you should have been trained a long time ago, psychic. It's a shame they didn't figure out what you were until recently."

I'd gotten to know the hellhounds well after our ordeal with the Collector, though my powers were also enough on their own to put me on their radar.

Melaina's gaze slid to Elias. "She's shadow drunk. Not an unusual occurrence for someone drawing too much energy at one time from the Infernum, but it is unusual for someone her age."

I giggled again, completely unable to control the urge to laugh. There was no way she was calling me old. I was only twenty-four.

"I know what shadow drunk is," Elias responded, petulant.

"Then you know—"

"I get it, hellhound," Elias cut her off.

Melaina shrugged, her face smug. "Just keep it contained, angel."

I was no longer listening to them, my body swaying to the music, my vision blurring. Shadows drew toward me like magnets. I found myself calling to them the same way I had when I was taken captive by the Collector. Then, while standing in a pitch-black room afraid for my life, the one holding me prisoner had told me not to be afraid, to use the spirits. I hadn't completely understood then, and I didn't completely understand now.

"Holy shit! It smells like the Infernum in here," a biker near me said, awed. By the insignia on the back of his leather vest, I knew he was a member of the local chapter of SIN, Swords of the Infernal Night. It was an outlaw motorcycle club that operated within town but kept its illegal business outside of it. The only reason I even knew about the club's dealings in the first place was because I'd been drawn into quite a bit of dark town business lately.

Harper Sinclair, now the girl everyone went to for help when things went wrong. Loyal. Dependable. Trustworthy. Safe.

"Don't be safe," the shadows told me. *"Be anything except safe."*

Inhaling deeply, I breathed in the smell of Hell, the smell of death and freedom. The golden light from the club around me transformed into a halo of blurred glitter, the world a beautiful kaleidoscope of sounds and bright colors.

There was a stage in front of me, a pole rising up from the floor, any dancers absent. Elias called my name, but I was too far gone to care. I just wanted to strip myself bare, literally, in front of the world.

"No more hiding," the shadows prompted.

I was so very, very tired of hiding.

I'd climbed the stairs, my hands yanking on my clothes, my body swaying against the pole, when the first whistles broke through. Yells of encouragement rose up from the crowd. I wasn't a splendid dancer, but I wasn't a terrible one either. It was the *removing the clothes* bit that was awkward.

The shirt went first, my clumsy fingers pulling the tight top I wore over my head. The bra beneath was red and lacy, and I toyed with the straps, my eyes closed as I made love to the music.

Using the body to express oneself was a splendid way to tell a story. I told stories every day with my fingers. I translated for the dead, writing words and beseeching requests, and snapped shots of other people's stories with my camera. My fingers were windows into other people's worlds.

Tonight, my body was the window into mine, my hands gliding down my flesh, enjoying the sensation. The shadows danced with me, and I didn't care who saw us. Right now, I was a queen of darkness, and I was enjoying the power. There was no room for embarrassment, no room for regret or doubt.

"More!" someone shouted. "Give us more."

I moved closer to a group of men sitting nearby, cash and drinks littering their table. One in particular, a blond with a cigarette hanging from his lips, crooked his finger. I obeyed the silent command. My eyes flicked to Elias, catching the way his jaw worked, before they went back to the unknown man who'd stepped to the edge of the stage.

The dark desire in the blond's gaze had me enraptured. My pulse pounded in my ears as I shimmied my way over—his head nearly even with my core as he looked up at me.

"Remove it," he said, a crisp Benjamin between his fingers, his eyes on my chest. The bra I wore snapped at the front between the breasts. Power surged through me. Not lust, not desire for this stranger, but power, because I could control this man with my body. I smiled, and a pale hand reached up and touched my thigh.

Somewhere from the back of the room I heard a growl I knew. *Elias.* My gyrations slowed, then dark whispers rose above everything else. "*Show him. Control him.*"

My attention returned to the man. He raised his brows and tapped the one-hundred-dollar bill against his chin as he waited. *Easy money.* I undid the clasp, letting my bra fall open.

"I think that's good," Elias's voice said suddenly from behind me, a large jacket enveloping me, the thick material covering the nakedness I'd bared.

A tear streaked down my cheek, the feel of it unexpected. Why was I crying?

"It's not nearly enough," I whispered. My head swung back to the blond. He was covered in shadows, and his face had turned hard.

Elias picked me up, using his body to shield me as he carried me off the stage and through the room, his breathing fast and hard, his voice husky when he said, "No, it's not nearly enough. It's damn well not nearly enough."

CHAPTER 7

ELIAS

*W*ith my jacket around her shoulders, I carried her toward the exit. I'd let her carry on for too long. She needed to have the freedom to find herself. I wanted that for her. Or, I had wanted that for her until her clothing became optional. *Holy fuck.* Her body radiated need. The spirits and demons had worked her into a frenzy, and though I hated the malevolent bastards, I wasn't immune to desire. Hell, the bulge in my pants had me limping as I pushed my way through the crowd.

"The lady didn't pick up her tip," a voice drawled from behind.

What the actual . . . I stilled, but didn't turn around. "Go back to the stage. Another dancer will be along to entertain you shortly."

The man grunted. "What if I don't want another dancer?"

Harper's flushed face lifted to mine, her eyes wide. I shifted her to my side, keeping one arm tightly around her back as I finally gave the man my full attention. "I don't give a rat's ass what you want."

His brown eyes flashed. Just my luck. This douchebag would have the balls to challenge me. Harper had worked her magic on this one. I could smell his need. He was two minutes from climax; all he needed was a willing body—or his hand.

Melaina caught my eye from near the bar, her face tight with irritation at the crowd building around us. One touch and I could have the man drooling over the biker sitting in the corner, if I wanted. I jerked my chin. It was time to leave.

Ignoring the cocky tourist who had no clue the shit he'd put himself in, I spun for the door and murmured to Harper, "Let's go."

I took one step, then everything happened in slow motion as Harper gasped and stumbled away from my side.

"Stay with me, darling," the man said. "I'll make those tears disappear."

His words didn't register half as much as the sight of his fingers wrapped around Harper's slender wrist. I lost my shit.

We flew across the space and slammed into a wall, his head bouncing at the impact. "You don't fucking touch her," I hissed, my face in his as my forearm locked across his neck. "I could crush you—"

"Elias?" Harper's small hands pulled at my hips, her body against my back. "Don't," she begged.

The blond turned red, his mouth moving like a fish out of water as he groped for words he wouldn't find, thanks to me.

A commotion broke out behind us, and Harper yanked at me again. "We need to leave. Now." Her voice was stronger this time, an order instead of a plea, and my anger tempered.

Shoving my weight against the blond once more, I released him. "Don't let me see you near her again. Got that?"

He nodded, rubbing at his neck. Bending down, I swiped the bill he'd dropped when I rushed him. Without looking for Melaina or her bouncers, I grabbed Harper's hand and hurried for the door.

I flicked the hundred toward the bouncer at the entrance. "For the trouble. Tell Melaina I'm sorry," I said as we stepped out into the cold night and toward an awaiting gondola.

"Out," I ordered the couple who had stepped into the lift right as Harper and I arrived. The man balked, and I released a low growl that had him pulling his companion back outside without another glance.

Fixing my gaze on the bouncer, I reached for the door handle myself. "Just us."

He gave me a nod as the door slammed shut. A moment later, the whir of the motors sounded, and we pushed away from the cliff.

I had ten minutes.

Shit. The sulfur scent of Hell had temporarily paralyzed me. I may be locked out of Heaven, but Hell was certainly no friend of mine. My very existence rebelled against everything Harper was so drawn to— she embraced the seduction of the darkness, and I longed to destroy it. By the time I talked myself down from the urge to dispatch the club of its less savory occupants—those species being the reason I didn't visit this place to begin with—Harper was sans shirt and tits flying. Then that asshole had touched her. Not once, but twice.

I spun Harper around and fisted her hair, pulling her head back until she met my gaze. "Tell me you want this."

Tears fell from her demon-fed black eyes as she blinked. She nodded.

I took a step forward, and she moved back.

"Tell me." I hated the anger in my voice, but siphoning off the massive amounts of darkness her demons had filled her with had me punchy. Somehow, one of the gifts I'd received upon my creation was the one thing a girl like Harper needed—everything she absorbed, I could pull away. It had taken a few coffee meetups with her before I'd noticed the way my power worked around her. I was like an antidote to her brand of poison. And her poison had just infected me. I'd almost killed a human . . .

I released Harper and shoved my hands through my hair. "Fuck!"

I'd attacked a man for touching her. *Not good.*

Harper's hiccupped sniffle settled me as she breathlessly admitted, "I want this."

Green returned to her eyes, and I released the lingering anxiousness in my tense limbs. I had been prepared to fight up there; my muscles had begged for it. In the eighteen years since Breckin was born and I'd taken over raising him, I'd somehow came to believe I'd become more human. More accepting to those species in this town who weren't on my side of the battle. To the stupidity of humans.

"*You have, angel. You didn't want to fight because there were damned in there. You wanted to fight because they looked at her.*" Never had her shadows been so right. "*She fuels your rebellion from Heaven.*"

My breaths came in shallow pants as I took another step forward. "Do you want me?"

"I do. I want you." Harper nodded and moved back again. Her retreat caused me to drop my hands. *She wants me, but she cowers?* I studied her tear-streaked face. It was a flushed, beautiful mess. "I need you, Elias."

She clutched the edges of my black jacket closed over her naked chest. I smiled and slipped my hand in, my fingers brushing her side. "Do *you* need me? Or is that the shadows speaking?"

"They don't—"

"Don't insult me by telling me they don't speak to you like that, Harper." My other arm wound around her backside and jerked her hips into contact with mine. "You let them control you. Yes, they are part of you, but you let them become you."

My palm skimmed up her ribcage and settled beneath her breast. Harper whimpered. "Tell me you want me to touch you." I stole a look out the window. "We have seven minutes."

She released her grip on my jacket and touched my jaw. "I want you to touch me."

With my gaze holding hers, my thumb slid over the soft curve of the underside of her breast and circled her nipple twice. Her eyes shifted left at my touch, and I palmed her. "Look at me."

She did. Our eyes held while I massaged her left breast, then dragged my hand across her breastbone and gave the right the same attention. The pad of my thumb flicking at her raised nipple coaxed another whimper from her lips. My jacket slipped from her shoulders, exposing her nakedness, as I leaned forward and used my hand against her chest to bend her backward over my arm at the base of her spine.

"Do you want my lips on you?" I murmured against the hollow of her neck.

She grabbed at my bicep with one hand and weaved her fingers into the hair at the base of my neck with the other. "I want everything, Elias. Your lips, your tongue, your—"

My tongue stopped her list.

I drew one puckered nipple into my mouth and pulled, my teeth nipping at her soft skin as the flat of my tongue suckled. Harper's nails drew across my scalp, holding me to her breast. The slight tang of her salty skin on my lips had me thrusting my dick closer to the heat between her legs. The air smelled like sex.

She was so fucking perfect. "You're beautiful," I said as I righted her. "I want you, Harper Sinclair."

Our mouths collided in a battle of dueling tongues. We were starved.

My larger body pushed until her back was against the glass of the gondola, her hand grabbing the rail as I removed my arm from behind her. Her pheromones were wildly alluring, her scent driving my hands up her thighs and under her skirt. My fingers rounded the curve of her ass and grazed the edge of lacy panties as Harper sucked in a sharp breath and caught my bottom lip with her teeth.

I pulled my head back in silent question. Her hips jerked forward in silent answer.

My middle finger found her heat first. "Fuck me," I mumbled.

Harper giggled. "Isn't that the point?"

Cupping her breast with one hand and toying with her folds with the other, I smiled and licked her lips once. "That is absolutely the point."

The lift slowed its descent. "Damn." I pulled my damp fingers from her panties.

"You've got five minutes to change your mind, if you want to," I said as I brushed one fingertip across her bottom lip. She surprised me by shifting forward and drawing it into her mouth, sucking her own taste from my hand.

I groaned when she let go. "Stingy girl, I'd planned on doing that."

"You can get down on your knees and taste me all you want, angel."

"In five minutes, I will." I sealed that promise with a kiss.

Harper giggled, still a little shadow drunk, as we pulled down my gravel drive, not a mile from Silk's parking lot. Before we'd initially passed my place on the way to the nightclub, I'd assumed she was directing me back to my house. Since my place was over the hangar that housed my helicopter and business, I lived in a relatively secluded area on the outskirts of town off County Road 13.

"Don't move," I warned, jumping out of the truck and going around to open her door.

She laughed for a second time as she slid to the ground, one hand still holding my jacket closed over her chest. "You weren't kidding about the five minutes."

I stood entirely too close as I stared at her upturned face. "It's only been three. I have two minutes left to get you inside and on my bed."

Her hand found mine at our sides. "Lead the way."

Harper Sinclair being assertive was not something the people of this town would expect. Then again—after her aborted striptease—their feelings about her were bound to change. I didn't bother giving her the grand tour of the place as we entered. It was simple enough. A stairway in the office of Ski-Ventures led upstairs to a spacious, yet cozy, open living space which consisted of one living room, dining room, and kitchen, along with two bedrooms, each with an en suite bath.

I closed the door and leaned against it, removing my shoes as Harper eyed the place. What did she think of it? It was a bachelor pad, but it was warm and lived in. Vivienne had even bought me a bunch of throw pillows for the couch, because she and Breckin had liked to visit me here when they needed to get away from Hamon and Rachel at the house.

I crouched down and touched Harper's calf.

"Foot?" I asked as she glanced over her shoulder. She lifted her leg from the floor, and I removed the shoe from her left foot, then her right, before standing and taking her hand. "Do you want a drink or anything?"

"Just directions to your bedroom." She glanced at her wrist, like she wore a watch. "You're down to one minute."

Her flirtatious grin had me laughing as I swiped a bottle of water from the counter and pulled her through my living room and down the small hallway to the master bedroom. When we stepped inside, I twisted the lid from the water bottle and took my time downing half the contents as I studied Harper standing in my bedroom. The hard-on that had barely deflated on the drive from Silk perked right back up. As if by design, she stood in the shaft of moonlight coming in from the uncovered windows that flanked my bed. Her fingers had gone to her hair, combing it up and out of her face, which left my jacket gaping open.

Everything about the way she looked, and what she had been through, sparked the protective nature in me. Her shadows worried me. They allowed her to be more direct and aggressive, but they also posed a danger to her. The man at the strip club was a perfect example. If I hadn't been there . . . It was danger like that I wasn't willing to risk. A danger I wanted to protect her from.

I held the water bottle out for her. After a pause, she took it.

"Now, what am I going to do with you?" My index finger drew a line down the naked skin peeking out from the open zipper. Harper shivered and took a sip of water. "I believe we were right about . . . here," I said as I touched the top of her skirt. I curved my fingers into the waistband and jerked her against my body. "I want to taste that sweet scent lingering on my fingers."

The water bottle fell to the floor as I shoved my jacket over her shoulders. Dropping to my knees, I pulled it down her arms. I trailed a circle of kisses around the silky skin of her stomach while I reached up and cupped one breast, then the other. Harper slipped back and fell to sit on the bed with a low laugh.

"How did you feel in that club, Harper?" I asked as I inched between her knees and took her face in my hands. "What did the shadow demons make you feel?"

"Freedom." Her hands worked at the buttons of my shirt. "Powerful." Her words turned me on even as they warned me away. She had the kind of power that could go very, very wrong if the shadows controlled her or if my enemies discovered what she was capable of.

I spread my arms until she freed me of my button-down and undershirt, then returned to exploring her exposed skin. My fingers traced her collarbone, over the peaks of her breasts, through the valley between them, and down along the ridges of her ribcage. Her skin was a maze, and I was following every path available down to the promised land.

"You *are* powerful." My thumbs slid into her waistband. "Just look at me. You put an angel on his knees. *I'm* on *my* knees for the privilege of worshiping you, my little *umbra amans*."

A rush of air expelled from her parted lips, but no words came. Instead she grabbed my face and kissed me deeply. Her nipples grazed my chest, our position awkward enough that we touched, but weren't skin to skin. I inched as close to her body as I could get. It wasn't enough.

"You make me feel freedom, too," she said between kisses. "You accepted me when I had no one. You weren't scared of what I am—"

I broke our kiss. I wasn't scared of what she was; I feared what that meant for her.

"Don't." Wrapping my arms around her waist, I pressed my face against the swells of her chest. "You are a beautiful soul, Harper Sinclair. You are powerful, and complicated, and . . . and you are not something to fear. Okay?" The words burned my throat and clutched at my heart, because I was working to convince myself as much as I was to convince her.

"Okay," she agreed softly, her mouth pressing to the top of my head.

Feeling weak and helpless in a way I had never known, I turned in to her skin and rained kisses across her chest. Harper's head rolled back, her eyes closing as I lavished each breast with all my attention before I gently pressed her backwards onto the bed. My hands made quick work of peeling her skirt and red panties down her legs. My mouth followed their trail, leaving wet kisses on the inside of her thigh, knee, calf, and ankle as I tossed the unneeded clothing across the room. When I stood to remove my own pants, my hands stilled at the waistband as I took in the temptress on my bed. My cock protested the holdup.

I unhooked my button and shoved the slacks to my knees. Harper rose to her elbows with a twinkle in her eyes. She licked at her lips, and the image of a starving animal ready to pounce upon its next meal came to mind. Harper looked famished. Or maybe that was me?

"Leaving on your boxers?" she asked.

I kicked my pants away and settled a knee on the bed. "For now." I tapped at her leg, nodding for her to move, and she crawled backward as I climbed over her, then settled between her knees. "I have a little business to attend to first."

"A little busin—" Her words cut off as I moved between her thighs.

The first swipe of my tongue—from her damp center to her clit—brought Harper's hand down on the covers beside me. Her nails scratched the fabric as she fisted my comforter. The second—executed with the flat of my tongue at a lazy pace—brought curse words.

"Elias?" My name was a plea on her lips.

I gripped her ass, and she clenched her thighs around my head as I lapped at her juices. "You taste like freedom to me."

Harper pulled my hair with a low "yes" when my tongue plunged deeper. A finger followed. Then two.

"Yes. Oh, God . . . shit."

I kissed her left thigh and lifted my head just enough to see her face. "You like that, huh?"

Her eyes were clenched tight, her head moving restlessly from side to side as my fingers pumped. I shifted my thumb to press against her clit, and Harper jerked at the touch. Her teeth bit into her bottom lip.

"Yeah, you like that, baby?" My voice was thick with desire. The woman was killing me.

Harper hissed, "Fuck me."

Smiling, I lowered my face and nipped at her thigh to keep my satisfaction with her response at bay. My temptress wasn't having that.

She yanked at my hair, pulling up my head and settling a wild and wickedly wanton look on me. "I want you to fuck me, Elias. Now."

I'd barely moved to my knees before Harper sat up and tugged my boxer briefs over my ass, her hand diving in to wrap around my very hard and very ready cock.

It was my turn to groan as she gripped me tightly, her thumb swiping at the bead of moisture on the head. "Shit," I said through gritted teeth.

She ran her hand from tip to shaft, alternating her hold from tender to death grip. My balls tightened with the urge for release. "Harper"—I sank my hand into her hair— "if you keep doing that . . ."

I didn't need to finish my sentence. She shook her head with a smile. "No way. I want to feel you deep within me when you get off."

My forehead dropped to hers. "Holy hell, how did we fight this for so long?"

"I honestly don't know."

Removing her hand from my member, I kicked off my boxers. I reached for the condom box I'd tossed in my bedside table this afternoon. Harper's brows knitted together as she watched me tear the package open.

"I bought these this morning. I don't sleep around, Harper. In fact, I've never slept with a woman in this bed. I just figured after last night . . ." I shrugged.

"I wasn't worried about that. I just . . . you're an angel, it's not like you have to worry about disease." If it were possible, I would have sworn her face had turned a brighter shade of red.

"No, but I can father Nephilim," I reminded her. "I raised one, remember? I might not be human, but I am a responsible guy."

Her thumbs pressed into my hips as she drew me forward and arched her hips. "I don't want responsible right now, I want—"

Lifting her ass higher, I slipped inside her in one smooth motion.

"Sex," Harper exhaled. I joined her husky moan with one of my own.

Her body clenched around mine—holding me tightly—as I withdrew, then sank back in. I dropped to the bed and covered her body with mine. My hands held her face still as I lowered my mouth to hers and kissed her slowly, my tongue moving at the same languid speed as our bodies. I wanted to take my time, to savor the feeling of friction building between us. I wanted to allow her body to suck every drop of life from mine. I could give that to her, I could give myself to her. Love her. Honor and protect her . . .

"Oh, fuck," I groaned as Harper shifted her hips and met me thrust for thrust. Her nails scratched at my back and pressed into my ass. Her whimpers shifted from gasps to exaltations.

I rose to my knees and increased my rhythm, my thumb rubbing circles around her clit as her breaths caught in her throat. She was close, her walls clenching and unclenching my length with each thrust. Her eyes had closed a while ago, and I joined her in that bliss. Letting our bodies form the pictures. Letting our ears take in the slapping sound of desire meeting desire. I inhaled the proof of our passion with every ragged breath—heat, salt, sex. It coated my lungs.

"Yes. Yes. Yes." Harper came with her fingers gripping my right knee. Her other hand had clutched the pillow she'd pushed out of her way at some point. Her body trembled as she sighed. A few thrusts later my release came, and I fell to her chest with a growl.

I sucked the salty sweat from her neck as I came down from the high. "I'm not done with you, Harper Sinclair. Not even close."

She stretched her limbs out beneath me, and I rolled to my side to give her room to breathe. After a moment, she propped her head up. "I would hope not."

My lips brushed hers before I shifted toward the edge of the bed. "Let me get rid of this and wipe off. I'll bring you something." A little of the vixen within had vacated in our post-sex haze. She offered me a small smile and looked a bit lost, her eyes failing to meet mine for more than a moment. "Crawl under the covers. I'll be right back."

"Under the covers?" Her eyes went wide as she pulled at my blankets. "I'm staying here?"

I couldn't help but notice the hopeful note in her tone. The condom and mess could wait. Angling myself away from the bed, I perched on the edge and touched her arm. "Harper?" She stopped her flurry of movement. "Of course you're staying here. Or, if you prefer, we could go to your place, but I see no reason to leave here when we're already dressed for bed. Either way, I planned on sleeping with you. This isn't a one night stand."

With a smile, Harper scooted the distance between us on her knees and kissed me.

"Why *did* we wait so long to act on this?" She asked the same question I'd asked right before I lost all concept of thinking when her hand touched my dick.

I gave her the same answer she had given. "I honestly don't know."

I brushed my knuckles over her cheek and went to the bathroom. When I returned with a washcloth for her, she was fast asleep. I stared at her, concern etching my brow.

Tonight, I'd seen her let loose for the first time, but I'd also seen what she was capable of, what her shadows were capable of doing to her. And what they might do to me.

"You can't have her," I told them fiercely. I'd spent the last year watching over Harper Sinclair. I'd spent the last year seeing her tackle a list of firsts she'd been too afraid to tackle when she was growing up because she feared hurting people. I didn't want the shadow demons to ruin what she'd accomplished.

But she'd also mentioned needing the shadows, as if their power was hers.

"I won't let you have her," I repeated.

"You don't have much choice," the shadows replied. *"We are a part of her, angel. This has to be up to her."*

CHAPTER 8

HARPER

"*Why did you do this to us, Harper? Why did you do this to yourself?*" the shadows screamed at me, the sound jerking me from sleep. My body was tangled in white sheets, the smell of popping bacon strong in the air.

My limbs were pleasantly sore, and I stretched, my hand falling on the empty space beside me. *Elias.*

His name had barely crossed my mind when the shadows appeared above me, larger and scarier than they had been in the past month. Like looming, hooded grim reapers ready to swallow me whole. They were pissed.

"*You betrayed us,*" they accused. "*Do you want us gone? Do you hate us that much?*"

My heart clenched, memories of the glorious night before suddenly tainted by the shadows' hurt feelings.

"Don't do this," I whispered.

My words were barely audible, but Elias heard them anyway.

"Are you hungry?" he asked from his kitchen.

I rolled from the bed, my gaze on the ghostly forms hovering near me. Their anger was a scary thing, dark and foreboding. It felt like being trapped beneath murky water, unable to breathe.

Elias's white button-down shirt from last night was laid out on the edge of his dresser, and I picked it up, his delicious scent comfortable and safe against my nose as I wrapped it around me. Pushing my arms into the sleeves, I buttoned it over my bra-less chest and lifted the collar to sniff the fabric.

Elias.

"Why, Harper?" the shadows asked, insistent. *"Why the angel?"*

I wanted to clasp my head in my hands to drown out their voices, but it wouldn't do any good. I loved the shadows, but I also cared about Elias in a way I'd never cared about anyone else before. *"Please,"* I mouthed, being careful not to speak aloud.

"You didn't have to cook," I said, exiting the bedroom.

Elias Jamison stood at the stove, shirtless, his jeans riding low on his hips. He was magnificent, the sight of him sending a renewed rush of desire straight to my core.

"There's hot cocoa on the bar," Elias informed me, his voice bright.

My gaze fell to a plain, sturdy brown mug, steam rising from the top. The shadows' sadness, anger, and betrayal stole my appetite.

"After everything we've done for you?" the shadows asked.

When I didn't say anything, Elias turned, his gaze finding my face. I knew by the way his muscles tensed that he sensed and heard the darkness.

He abandoned what he was doing, setting the breakfast he'd cooked aside. It seemed like such a waste sitting there untouched, but I couldn't make myself offer to eat the food or drink the cocoa.

"Let's sit," Elias suggested.

I followed him to his couch.

Curled into the cushions of his deep sofa, I reclined against the armrest.

He pulled a folded blanket off the footrest and draped it over my legs. "If only you knew how delicious you look right now . . ." He smiled. "This blanket is for your safety, not mine."

My grin answered his. "And if I don't want to be safe?"

"We could have kept you safe," the shadows wailed, invading the sweet moment. *"You're hurting us all."*

My smile fell. I'd chosen to sit in a way that kept me from getting too close because I'd already upset the shadows enough. Even so, I felt like I was suffocating.

Elias took the middle spot on the couch, lifting my feet to place them in his lap.

Chewing the side of my lip, I tucked my legs in closer, removing my feet from him.

He sighed. "What's going on in that head of yours, Harper?"

I encircled my legs with my arms and settled my chin on my knees. Hesitant. How did you tell the person you were falling in love with that your head was full of hate? The shadows wanted nothing more than to separate us. Which meant they'd constantly be attacking him.

Elias threw his head against the back cushion and looked up at the ceiling. "Do you want to know why I drove to your house Friday night at three a.m.? Why I couldn't even wait until morning to see or call you?"

Relief and curiosity overwhelmed me. Relief, because I had time to gather my thoughts. Curiosity, because I sensed this was something that had been plaguing his mind.

"There are things you don't know about me."

"You've been around for an eternity. I imagine there are a lot of things I don't know." He turned his head at my light tone.

"True." His hand snuck under the blanket and settled against the back of my calf. Warm. Comfortable. "But there are things you should know, if we're going to . . ." He trailed off.

What? Continue this relationship? Remain friends?

"I'm pretty sure I understand all about being complicated, Elias." The shadows gathered along the walls, and even though they didn't have defined facial features, I knew they were sneering at me.

He gave my leg a squeeze. "I've lived an unconventional life, for an angel, for a really long time. I wasn't meant for Earth, but I chose my path, forsaking my place in Heaven because a friend needed me.

"I've cared for very few things during my existence. Angels were made to worship only one, but He gave us free will and, because of that, I formed bonds that would never break. Not even in death."

Leaning further back into the corner of the couch, I relaxed. A little too much. Drawing so much on the shadows' energy the night before and allowing them to draw on mine had sapped me of strength. Even after sleeping a few hours, I was tired. "Breckin's father?"

"Hamon is one, then Breckin. There were two other angels: one who betrayed us all and one who forfeited her angelic existence out of guilt, because she couldn't help him—they are both gone now. Our bonds made his betrayal harsher and her loss unbearable."

"What happened?"

His jaw tightened and I longed to touch it, to soothe the pain there. "Our history is a mess of wars and betrayals, some we won and others we lost. Revenge was had, but peace is not something we've found."

I listened intently. Listening was something I'd always been good at. *Too* good. Being a good listener kept people from asking questions.

"I stepped away from my duties long ago. After Phaedra was stripped of her angelic being, she was basically rendered human. I dedicated my time to protecting her. Hamon sacrificed himself, pretending to be something he isn't, so that we might stay safe and hidden away. It worked for a time, but our demons always find us, don't they?"

He shook his head and drew my feet into his lap again, tucking the blanket around them. I didn't withdraw this time.

"The betrayals of our past haven't gone away. When Breckin found Vivienne, it opened a whole new problem. That's why Hamon and I left so quickly after the incident with the Collector. We tracked some fallen who'd been hunting Breckin and Viv. We ended them, but there will be more." Sitting forward, he angled his body toward me. "There's always more. Giving in to my feelings for you, giving in to my desires, could make you a target."

"I don't understand. Why—"

"You live in a town full of the supernatural, Harper. You yourself are unique. Hamon and I are angels. This isn't a fight between two shifter species, or for magic, or power. Demons and angels, Heaven and Hell . . . our fight is for the world. For eternity."

"But you're not a part of that life. You don't have duties—"

"I have an allegiance to my creator, to Heaven. If I were called upon, I would return, and I would fight."

I inhaled deeply, my worries momentarily forgotten. "Why are you telling me this? Are you leaving again?"

"I'm not going anywhere." He massaged my feet, his thumbs applying deep pressure to the arches. "I told you because the last time I cared about someone, she was taken from us."

I flinched.

"Phaedra was like a sister to me; we were not romantic," he added, as if he sensed my jealousy. "Harper"—his serious gaze caught mine— "something nagged at me the other night. No . . . not something. It was one of your shadows. It was waiting for me when I arrived home. It reminded me of my mistakes. The way I left you here, alone. My failure to protect Phaedra. That's why I drove to your door, through a snowfall, at three a.m. I'd had a horrible feeling. I have this fear of losing you," he confessed.

I stared at Elias, his words squeezing my chest, my heart fluttering. He, like all the angels I'd met, was complicated. To live an eternity meant seeing and hearing things no one else ever had. I couldn't help but wonder why the men I'd let closest to me in life were angels. Maybe it was because, deep down, I knew they were the kind of beings I may never fully understand. The kind of beings part of me may never accept.

Maybe that was the fascination. Maybe *my* complicated being introduced to an even *bigger* complicated was my fate in life. If I was going to go with a complicated relationship status, Elias was definitely the way to go. No matter how fierce he looked or what kind of dangers knowing him might bring, he was a genuinely nice guy, the kind of guy a girl could trust with her heart.

Behind him, my shadows loitered near the ceiling at the back of the room, watching.

I stared back at them, my heart hurting. Why did seeing the dark spirits keep their distance make me feel sad and lonely? As if I was trying to end my friendship with them in favor of a relationship with

Elias. A friendship I had to admit I didn't want to give up. Something about the shadows made me feel whole.

"You look thoughtful," Elias murmured. "It's hard to read you sometimes."

My gaze edged back to his, the curiosity burning in his eyes making me shiver.

Under the blanket I'd pulled over myself, I touched my side. There was a small scar there, a reminder of how deep my connection to the shadows went. I'd let the spirits inhabit me once, similar to a possession, so that I could use their power, only to have them rip free of my skin when I couldn't control them. Elias had worshiped that scar last night, kissing circles around it.

The shadows understand you, I told myself.

"I'm sorry," I said suddenly, the apology flowing thickly off of my tongue. I'd had too little sleep last night. Even as important as this moment was, I couldn't seem to hold on to it. Sleep was a villain waiting to steal me away. "What I did Friday night. Attacking you . . ."

"No apologies," Elias said, a gentle smile on his face. "I think it's safe to say we have some things we need to work out."

Exhaustion, deep and intense, invaded my body, dragging down my eyelids and weighing down my limbs.

"I obviously wore you out," Elias whispered as his hands continued massaging my feet. "Nap, Harper."

He watched me, his gaze passing from me to the walls beyond. I think, on a deeper level, he may have sensed my warring thoughts, even if he didn't understand them.

Elias leaned toward me. "What are the shadows to you now, Harper?"

Sleep made my tongue drunk and loose. "Family," I answered.

I wanted to take it back as soon as I said it. Maybe it was better to tell him now before things got too twisted.

"I'm a demon," I whispered.

Elias frowned, but I saw the knowledge in his gaze, the truth he wanted to ignore. "You're a psychic with a link to the Infernum, not a demon."

"It's much deeper than that. Because of the circumstances of my birth, I'm a demonic human."

There. I'd said it.

"Most importantly, your parents were *human*," he insisted. "Demon connection or not, you can choose to ignore the dark side."

Sleep, and the way it weakened my defenses, was not my friend. I blinked it back.

"Harper?" Elias prodded. "Why do they hate me so much? Your shadows?"

The vulnerability in his voice tugged at my heart. "Because they're scared of you. They're afraid that me being with you will make me push them away."

"Is that such a bad thing?" he asked, genuinely curious.

I looked at the shadows. "You know what they are. They were terrible people when they were alive. The ones who were human, anyway. They sold their souls to the Infernum, and none of them expected to find redemption or affection in the afterlife. Until they found me. I care about them, and they don't want to give that up. *I* don't want to give that up. Th . . ." My words trailed off, and I narrowed my eyes, frustrated at my weariness.

"Th . . ." I tried again, but exhaustion finally got the better of me, carrying me away, sending me reeling into a dark world I was more than comfortable in lately.

My words hung in the air, bridging reality and dreams. *I don't want to give that up.*

Strange how the truth a person doesn't want to admit to themselves comes out when he or she least expects it to.

I didn't want to ignore the darkness. I liked how comfortable it was. Like a warm fire on a cold winter night. Or a grilled cheese sandwich and a cup of hot chocolate.

I awoke back in Elias's bed, the early afternoon sun filtering in through a picture window, a carpet of blinding white snow sparkling in the mountainous world beyond.

The house was too quiet, the shadows too calm, and I knew by their behavior that Elias was gone.

My head rolled to the side, my gaze landing on a note left behind on Elias's pillow.

Harper,

I'm sorry. There was an emergency on the mountain with some skiers. I'll be home as soon as possible. My truck keys are on the counter if you need to leave. Help yourself to anything you need.

Love, Elias

Relief washed over me, not because there was something going on in the mountains, but because Elias hadn't abandoned me because of the confession I'd made.

CHAPTER 9

ELIAS

*I*t was late afternoon by the time I returned to Havenwood Falls after flying a rescue mission out on Mount Sousa. *Damn tourists.* As secluded as our little town was, due in large part to the Court and magical wards used to keep the town safe, we still allowed a good number of high rollers to vacation here—especially during ski season—to keep the local economy pumping. This morning's rescue was just that: big-city daredevils who didn't pay attention to the mountain conditions. The fact that those egocentric pricks pulled me away from Harper chapped my ass. Walking out my door after our revelations this morning was tough. And now here I was, enduring the Winterfest crowds in search of her, because she'd left my house.

"Did you think she'd stay? Did you think she'd choose you over us?" The warning scraped across my forehead, and I looked over my shoulder at the little shadow friend I'd picked up, thanks to Harper. His smoky form flitted about, encircling tree trunks and slinking along the slush-and-snow-covered sidewalks, as he followed me. He'd lingered in my presence all day.

In that vulnerable moment between wakefulness and sleep earlier, she'd called the shadows her family. Why had she made that connection? Yes, she was tied to demons because of the circumstances surrounding her birth, but *she* wasn't a demon.

"Or is she?" The shadow's question tickled my skull.

"No," I said aloud, then ducked my head as a group of high schoolers stopped and stared. I lifted a wave and kept walking. *I would know if she were a demon. I would sense it,* I justified in my head. Then I cursed, because I'd felt the need to reply at all. *Damn creature.*

I considered crossing the street and heading into the Haven Saloon for the sole purpose of getting drunk—if only angels could get drunk —when a small, tightly bundled-up figure appeared from around the gazebo. The dark hair spilling out from beneath her red knit hat and over her puffy white jacket gave her identity away as much as the camera plastered to her face. Harper rotated in a slow circle, her index finger snapping away at the festivalgoers enjoying day two of Winterfest.

I shoved my hands into my pockets and watched, mesmerized by her focus as she pointed and clicked over and over. The joy on her face was undeniable, giving her a youthful quality that was enchanting. I was thirty yards away, but the click of each shot she took reached my angel ears. My gaze followed her lens, curious as to what had caught her attention.

When peals of laughter tore through the air, Harper lowered the camera, then crouched and began snapping again. Three young girls had entered the square hand in hand, their faces bright red from the cold, their bodies skipping and dancing in circles as they kicked at the thick snow on the ground and sang songs I didn't know. I envied their carefree exuberance. Their safe human existence.

Somewhat uncomfortable at the unusual jealousy blooming in my chest, I shifted and looked for Harper once more—only to find her camera lens pointed at me.

I drew a short breath.

The camera lowered an inch, and dark brows arched above sparkling green eyes.

"She could cost you your redemption, angel. Stay away," the shadow whispered.

"I can't," I murmured. My legs brought me toward the bewitching woman who'd stolen my affection. I knew this was a dangerous game. I'd stayed alone for a reason, but it was like I had no control where Harper Sinclair was concerned.

Memories assaulted me, images of the past year spent with her. The conversations we'd had over coffee and hot chocolate, the texts we'd shared, and the fights we'd survived.

And now I understood. I knew why Phaedra had risked her salvation to save Andras. I knew why Hamon lived with such hatred after her loss. Why I followed my best friends and left our birthplace. Why Breckin and Vivienne sacrificed their lives to be together.

Love. This was love.

Let this woman ruin me. Let her darkness do its best at breaking me down. I would fight for her. I was already fighting for her against an enemy I was afraid to lose to—herself.

Harper stood as I neared, a sweet smile on her lips, and lowered her camera to hang around her neck by the strap she wore. "Hey."

I didn't answer, my mind preoccupied by the sound of her heartbeats accelerating, the awareness that shot through me at the sight of her, and the warnings I was receiving from her shadow demon.

Her boot-covered feet shuffled back as I bore down on her, a man on a mission. "Elias?"

At the sound of my name, Desi's handle popped up out of the backpack Harper carried him around in.

I stopped just short of knocking her down and wrapped my arm around her back, my hand drawing her against my body. Leaning down, I touched my lips to her temple.

"Hey," I said, my mouth lingering on her chilled skin.

Her face turned into my touch, as though seeking the warmth my angelic skin provided.

"I'm sorry I left without saying goodbye." I kissed her cheek—right at the edge of her lips—worried anything more would lead to an embarrassing make-out session, then relinquished her.

Harper shook her head. "There was trouble on the mountain?"

"Skiers stranded—no injuries—but it took a while to find them."

Her gaze volleyed as she shifted in the space between my arm, still around her back, and my chest.

A light breeze blew her hair across her face, and I reached up to brush away a piece that stuck to her cheek. "I see you went home. You didn't feel like looking sexy and lounging in my dress shirt all day?"

"I needed to get out and get some fresh air."

There were too many unspoken sentiments in that statement. "We need to discuss the shadows." Harper's grip tightened on her camera strap, and I ran a finger over her white knuckles. "Can we go back to my place? I'll make you dinner," I teased.

"Grilled cheese?"

Her simple request brought a smile to my face. "Damn, how'd I get so lucky? I just happen to have all those ingredients in my kitchen." I held out my hand. "C'mon, gorgeous. I'll throw in all the hot chocolate you can drink, giant marshmallows included." Things I kept on hand these days, thanks to Vivienne.

The sun had set over the mountains by the time I'd fed Harper, and we moved outside, where I stoked up a large fire in the pit beyond my hangar door. Unease grew between us. The longer I put off talking about the shadows, the thicker the tension became.

I couldn't sit across the fire from her and admire her pretty profile as she stared off into the mountains all night. I had to speak.

"Last night at Silk," I began, "what happened with me and that guy . . . that can't happen again. That's not me."

Harper glanced at the fire, the flames dancing in her eyes. It suited her. "I know." Her gaze flicked to me. "What set you off like that?"

I scoffed. "Besides a stranger lusting after you?"

A smile tugged at her lips. "Besides that."

How did I explain this? Leaning forward in my seat, I rested my elbows on my knees. "Have you never noticed how my powers work when I'm around you? How I take your edge off? From the first time we met, I sensed the darkness surrounding you. It was like your energy had its own frequency, and it called directly to my abilities. You came around, and my angel senses lit up. I was created to draw all that iniquity burdening your soul away.

"The problem is, the more of your shadows I fight off, the more consumed I become." I tugged at the hair on my cheeks and stared into the flames.

It seemed symbolic somehow that we were separated by fire.

Harper's expression grew pained. "I feel less heavy when you're around." A sad laugh escaped. "You take my edge off, and I cause you trouble."

I closed my eyes at the defeat in her voice. "I can rid you of them. You know I have that ability. It would be simple." More than simple.

I reopened my eyes, curious for her reaction. It was what I'd expected. Shock, pain, maybe even a little revulsion. Unsurprisingly, she was surrounded by inky silhouettes, their murmurs low as they kept their distance.

"I haven't done that," I reminded her, lest she forget. "I've only used my gifts to banish them when they were a danger to you. I know you feel as though you need them. I don't understand it, but I know where you stand. I care about you enough to respect your wishes."

Harper's gaze was guarded, a look she'd worn her entire life.

"What I'm asking is that you understand my place here. I'm an angel in . . . who's falling for a summoner. I don't care. I'll deal with the bastards all day, every day if it means I get you. But if you don't rein them in and control them, they will turn dangerous. To everyone." I stood and circled the firepit slowly, giving her time to argue if she chose. "You don't have to get rid of them. You just need to control them."

Harper looked at me, her green eyes huge. "Now understand my position. I haven't lived a lifetime, and I admit I don't have the type of control I should, but when the only thing you've ever had to depend on is darkness, it makes the light harder to look at. When people have spent so long being afraid of you that you even start fearing yourself."

"I'm not afraid of you, Harper Sinclair." I squatted down in front of her chair. "Depend on me."

"I don't want to hurt you."

I rocked forward, my palms running up her jeans-clad thighs until the tips of my fingers were close enough to tease her center. "Does it look like I'm being hurt here?" I gripped her hips and tugged her forward in her chair. "Babe, if this is your definition of hurt, please, hurt me."

Harper's mouth parted in a silent *O* and white puffs of air mingled between us for one . . . two . . . three breaths before she fisted the collar of my shirt and fell forward from her seat. With her mouth on mine, I landed back first on the cold concrete with my little shadow lover straddling my lap.

Last night we'd made love, our pace slow, exploring. This was the opposite. This was hands tearing at buttons, teeth clashing, arms wrestling. This was Harper grinding into my rock hard erection until I dug my fingers into her hip flexors to pause the torture.

Harper lifted all of five inches from my mouth, a frown on hers. I bucked up and sucked her pouting bottom lip into my mouth, pulling a lusty groan from her throat.

"I'll fuck you out here all spring, summer, and fall, but your ass will be numb and your tits will freeze off in this weather. Since I happen to be extremely fond of these"—my hands tweaked her breasts —"could we move this inside?"

Harper giggled and agreed.

The reprieve didn't last long. She stripped as she led me up the stairs and into my bedroom, looking over her shoulder the entire way to verify that each piece of her abandoned clothing was matched with something of mine.

She took my dick in her palm the moment we reached my bed. "You want me to exercise control?" she asked, a hint of aggression flashing over her features.

I raised my arms in surrender. "I'm all yours."

It was a good thing I was immortal because this woman could kill me.

Harper wasted no time, rolling a condom on me before she slid her wet folds down my shaft with a relieved sigh.

I bit my lip and swallowed every curse known to man at the absolutely exquisite feeling of her body riding mine. Her head dropped forward as she pressed up on her knees, then sank down on my dick.

I fisted her long hair with one hand and circled her clit with the other.

Harper cursed, then twisted her hips. I nearly blacked out.

"Look at me," I ordered as I pulled at her hair again.

Her flushed face met mine, but she didn't stop moving over me.

"Do you see me?" I asked. Her eyes widened in answer. "Not good enough. Do you see me, Harper?"

My thumb applied a little more pressure to her clit, circling. "Yes," she gasped.

"Am I hard to look at?"

Her head shook. Not in answer, but in confusion.

I growled and yanked her arms, which were anchored on my chest for leverage, out from beneath her. Her chest fell forward, and I wrapped my arms around her back before flipping us over without losing our intimate connection.

"Am I hard to look at?" I asked again. I lifted her hips and sunk into her body as deeply as I could. "Does my light bother you?"

Recognition at her own words being thrown back at her hit, and she dug her nails into my ass, holding me still when all my body wanted to do was withdraw and slam its way back in. "I see you, Elias."

Her hold released, and I slipped my palm beneath her knee and shifted it toward her chest. The move changed my angle. Harper's head tossed from side to side on my pillow, her hand clenching my bicep as I quickened my thrusts.

"I want you to trust me," I told her. "I need you to know I won't desert you. I'm not afraid of you."

I believed in her innate goodness, but I also knew how strong the darkness was within her. *Even the devil was an angel once.* The sentiment had never failed to remind me of how precarious the battle between Heaven and Hell was. And I wouldn't forget how close she was to both sides—her beautiful soul and her hellbound fierceness.

I sunk forward and hid my face in the crook of her neck as my balls grew tight and release found me. Harper murmured and gasped, her hips riding out the waves of my orgasm, then following up with one of her own not a minute later.

It was only after I'd collapsed on my side and Harper had fallen asleep that I allowed myself to acknowledge that the aggression in our coupling—on both our sides—as mind-blowing as it was, had been fueled by her darkness.

CHAPTER 10

HARPER

Sleep was a double-edged sword for me. It gave me the chance to rest, but it also thinned the veil between reality and my subconscious. It made me more vulnerable to the darkness within, and to the temptation it wrought.

This was the reason I'd begun sleepwalking. Not the kind of sleepwalking that caused problems or put me in danger. So far, I'd never left my house. On some level, I wasn't even fully asleep. I knew what I was doing, but I couldn't stop it. Or maybe it was that I didn't *want* to stop it. It was more like my brain's free time to leave me messages to myself, making me aware of the things I fought to ignore when I was awake. And because I was a spiritual writer by birth, those messages usually came in words. Such as a red lipstick message on a mirror or a dry erase marker on the refrigerator.

I knew the moment I woke up that my world was about to come crashing down.

The last few days had been a high for me, a shadow-drugged binge that let me experience more emotions than I'd experienced in my entire life. All at once.

And the person who had been there to carry me, the one who'd seen me through the chaos, was Elias Jamison.

He was sitting next to the bed when I opened my eyes, his hard gaze on my face. There was no softness to his expression, but there was a softness to his eyes. It was his eyes I was trusting my heart with.

"I think we need to talk," Elias said, reaching out to push my hair off of my face.

My heart broke, and somehow I knew it was my fault.

"What did I do?" I asked.

"You told the truth," the shadows said, satisfied.

Rather than wait for Elias's response, I sprang from his bed, making a beeline for his bedroom door. My body knew just where to take me. Which meant one thing.

I'd left him a message.

Pausing in his kitchen, I let my mouth fall open. *Oh, Harper! What have you done?*

There, written in marker, were the words, "Go to hell. The darkness is my sanctuary. Release me to it."

The message was cold, cruel, and completely unlike me. It was my handwriting, but the words were rougher, the strokes I'd made with the marker bolder than usual.

But, deep down, I knew they were my words. I knew what I had written was even how I felt to some extent.

I'd said to him what I'd been wanting to say to the world. But to Elias, because of what he was and because of what we'd shared, it had to feel like a knife stab through the heart. The way he'd begged me to trust him, to look at him . . .

A tear slipped down my cheek.

"You did nothing wrong," the shadows whispered, their dark forms creeping into the space. *"Walk away from him, Harper."*

"Get out of my house!" Elias roared from behind me, having obviously followed me to his kitchen. "You aren't welcome here."

He had every right to be angry, every right to send them away. This was his house, his space. Not mine. But the shadows were part of me now. In a way, I was part of them. Images of the two of us making love, the wild way I'd let go of myself, ran through my head, and I placed a fist against my mouth. I'd never felt like this before. Not with anyone except Elias.

That was part of the problem.

"Get away from him!" Whatever warmth I received from the spirits was gone. Their anger, their hatred, was palpable.

I touched the scar on my side, the place where the shadows had once ripped out of my skin. "I-I . . ."

The shadows weren't weak. They were fierce, completely capable of controlling me as much as I was capable of controlling them. Only the way they acted now around Elias—agitated and inconsolable—made it hard for me to get a handle on them.

Words wouldn't come. Sobs tore out of me instead, the racking tears completely shaking my body. I had never been cruel before.

"I don't know whether to be pissed or sad," Elias said. "Did you mean that?"

I didn't turn around to see if he was looking at the words. Because if I looked at him, what I had to say next would be harder.

"Yes." But not the way he thought. "I'm not good for you."

"Bullshit. They're lying to you, Harper. They hate me. They want you all to themselves."

"We're not the ones trying to change who she is, angel."

My shoulders slumped. The shadows weren't lying, as much as I hated to admit it. Elias wasn't trying to change me, but when I was around him, I kept trying to change myself anyway. For him. Even if he wasn't asking it of me. And that, in itself, was exhausting. "I'm tired of holding it back. It hurts me to pretend I'm not part demon. It hurts me to pretend I'm not a summoner. It makes me act worse and raises the chance of me hurting someone if I hold it back, because then it just builds up."

"Dammit," Elias gripped the back of his head. "I'm not asking you to cover up who you are! I love who you are, but you can't let them control you, Harper." His words were a repeat of the night before.

"No." Inhaling, I choked back my tears. "I have to quit pretending the shadows aren't my responsibility. I've tied them to me, and I am responsible for them."

I turned toward him. "You make me feel good, Elias. You make me feel better about what I am, but you also make me feel guilty." There it was. The honest truth. "You make me feel guilty for wanting to invite the darkness in."

Elias stood before me, magnificent in only a pair of low-slung blue jeans. "That's not my intention. That's . . . I can help you."

The shadows screamed, the sound of their wails so loud, I fell to my knees, my hands gripping my head. "Stop."

This wasn't helping. The shadows' reaction to Elias was hurting me. "They're hurting me because of you," I said.

"You'll be stronger if you walk away," the shadows assured me. *"We can keep you safe. You need us, not him."*

Elias fell to his knees and grabbed my arms. "I'm trying to understand this. I've seen creatures, good and evil of every kind, but you have changed the rules of what you are. These spirits and demons do not belong to you; they belong to the Infernum. How can you trust them?"

I ignored Elias and concentrated on the shadows' arguments. "They're going about it all wrong."

Elias frowned. "What are you talking about? Going about what wrong?"

"Protecting me."

Elias inched forward. "Demons don't protect people, Harper."

"These do. They protect me." I didn't mean to sound argumentative, but my words came out defensive and hard. These demons had stayed with me even after my ordeal with the Collector. They'd been there when I screamed in my sleep and woke up covered in sweat, my heart a beating drum in my chest. I owed them a certain amount of loyalty.

Elias's gaze darkened, his voice lowering as he fell back to sit on the floor. "Is that what it feels like?" He paused, studying me. "I'd know if you were possessed."

"Then you know I'm not." I wasn't possessed. The shadows weren't here to use me. Were they? They wanted me to use them. I just hadn't quite figured out how to do it safely.

"You're not a bad person," Elias told me, his tone certain, as if he needed to convince himself.

"Say it!" the shadows yelled. *"Admit it!"*

The words poured out of me before I had the chance to hold them back. Deep down, I didn't want to admit what I knew I needed to face. I *liked* what I was becoming. "You don't have to be a bad person to want bad things."

I expected Elias to jerk back, to use this moment to completely break away from me, but he surprised me by staying firmly in place. He dipped his head and locked his gaze on mine. "What kind of bad things are we talking about?"

"Depends on if we're talking about the bedroom or in general." I'd gone from defensive to suggestive. And it felt *good.*

"Don't try to distract me, Harper. Not now," Elias said firmly. "Speaking of, I'd like to make love to you, Harper, not your shadows. Is that unreasonable?"

"You haven't made love to the shadows. I haven't let them in enough for that. Would you like to see what it's like when I really let them in?" There'd only been one time when I'd allowed the shadows complete entry into my body. I'd been a prisoner of the Collector and afraid of losing the people I loved.

"Do it!" the shadows cried gleefully. They lived for this.

"Don't," Elias warned.

"Let us in, Harper. We'll take care of him."

I pounded the floor with my fists. There were too many voices in my head. Too many things both the shadows and Elias wanted from me. It was all too much. "I can't learn to control them when you're around."

Elias stared at me. "I can—"

"No, you can't. Not with the way they feel about you." I wasn't choosing the shadows over Elias. I was choosing to control this on my own so that I could invite Elias into my chaos.

I was tired of being a risk. Some demons did have hearts. At least this demonic human did, because I could feel it breaking.

I'd never felt this way about anyone, not even the fallen angel who'd swept into my life more than a year ago. Lucas Fox had been exciting, different, and new. Wise in ways I would never understand.

But it was Elias who had called to my soul. Even then. The moment he'd locked eyes with me on the sidewalk outside Coffee Haven a year ago, right before my first demonic experience since childhood, I'd known he was different.

Elias was the one who stayed. Elias was the one who helped me accomplish my list of firsts. Elias was the one who sent me texts of encouragement when I needed to be a hero. Elias was the friend who never pushed. He simply offered.

I'd depended on him too much.

"I need to help myself." My words were shaky, but honest.

What I really wanted to say was, "I love you, Elias. I love you so much I need to figure myself out so I can love you the way you deserve." But I didn't say that, because I was afraid he wouldn't let me leave.

Elias dropped his head, his hands working their way into his pockets. The way we were now was nothing like we'd been the night before. I saw the worry on his face. He was having doubts, too, but his need to protect me was stronger than his misgivings. Which meant I needed to be the one to push away.

I'd never felt so vulnerable and yet so true to myself. I was letting Elias see a part of me no one else had ever seen. Even my Aunt Eloise.

"Take me home?" I asked quietly.

Elias nodded.

Leaving me, he entered his bedroom and returned fully clothed, my clothes in his fist. He pulled my shirt over my head, then handed me my jeans. "I'll take you home."

He walked toward the door and stopped. His spine stiffened as he looked at his ruined wall.

"Hey, Harper?" His voice broke, and he cleared his throat. I couldn't make a sound, and Elias looked over his shoulder. "Just so we're clear, you're the one doing the abandoning here. I was willing to stay."

He opened the door and disappeared down the stairs.

I had never felt so broken.

CHAPTER 11

ELIAS

Go to hell. The darkness is my sanctuary. Release me to it.

Two days later, Harper's words remained scrawled across my kitchen wall in bold black marker. And, as if that wasn't enough of a kick to the groin, she'd also left a friend behind.

"An angel and a demon." The shadow demon taunted me day and night. *"Tell me your real fear, angel?"*

"That I'll never have another moment of peace." I sank lower on my couch. "Would you get the hell out of here?"

I'd angled the couch toward the wall so I could see Harper's truths on display whenever I needed reminding. Instead of strengthening my resolve, it served to weaken it. I refused to believe that she thought we weren't good together. I refused to believe that two nights of passion was all we would ever have.

The demon floated toward the wall with a sort of snickering laugh. *"She wasn't wrong. I know your truest fears, angel. You cannot hide them from my kind."*

"Yeah? What's that?"

"You killed her."

For a moment, I was confused. Then the *her* he meant came into focus. He wasn't speaking of Harper. No, he was tearing at the bandages of my past. Ripping the hastily sewn seams loose.

Phaedra—she was my one true weakness. Or she had been, before Harper.

Sitting forward, I dropped my forearms to my knees and grabbed my head. "Clever little bastard, aren't you?"

"They will want to use her powers for their purpose. She is strong, but she is alone."

His warning was clear. He didn't mean the shadow demons that haunted her, although they were problematic. He meant others. The fallen ones, higher-class demons, even some residents of our town— the ones you wouldn't trust with your worst enemy—would be interested in the girl with the power to channel spirits and demons. And they would especially be interested in using her ability to possibly find a way to open a portal to the Infernum. Harper's skill set, even when she was at her weakest, was dangerous. The more self-aware she became, the scarier she was.

"What do you care? You and your damned friends wanted me out of her life . . ." I shut my mouth. Why in the hell did I continue to argue with these contradictory creatures?

"You could join us, angel. Feed the darkness of the world," the shadow hissed.

In this moment, with my heart shattered and strewn about the floor, the offer was more appealing than I cared to admit. I took the glass sitting on the floor at my feet and threw it across the room. The shadow disappeared.

I picked up my phone again and again over the next few days, wanting to text Harper. Her shadow demon had not returned to my place since I threw an empty scotch glass at its inky little body. I almost missed the guy. One thing he'd said replayed in my mind: *"She is strong, but she is alone."*

It was like these creatures truly *did* care about her. His comment wasn't a warning to goad me into anger or pain; it felt more like his own thoughts. Like he knew that Harper couldn't handle herself alone forever. She was so much more capable than she knew, but even the strongest beings needed someone at their side. Wasn't that what I'd tried to convince Hamon of for years after he set his vendetta into action, alone? He survived, but at what price? What was the price for my mistakes? Andras and Phaedra were gone. Breckin and Vivienne were hunted.

I wanted to protect her. That was all. The shadows wanted to protect her, too. I could finally admit that, as hard as it was. They didn't want her to be alone. They just didn't want *me* with her. Unless I gave in to the darkness.

And that I would not do. I was made of light. But I could embrace her darkness. If she'd let me.

CHAPTER 12

HARPER

$\mathcal{I}$ was perched on the side of a snow-covered cliff holding a camera, my gaze on the mountains before me, when the pain of the last few days hit me. The wind ran its cold fingers through my hair, the lightly falling snow stinging my cheeks. Winter in Havenwood Falls was as brutal as it was beautiful.

The shadows that trailed me swept up into the air, hovering. They were euphoric because they thought they'd won.

Staring up at them, I breathed the frigid air into my lungs and braced myself.

"You're angry," they said. It wasn't a question. They stated it because they knew they were right.

"You did the same thing that everyone else has done to me," I told them. "You think you know so much about what's right for me that it's clouding what is *actually* right for me."

My voice rose on the word *actually*, and it echoed off of the mountains.

Desi lay in the snow in the distance watching. He was only there to observe unless something went wrong. Today, I was working on controlling the shadows, even if it meant I was hurt in the process. Because I needed to get control of them before I saw Elias again, before I confessed how I really felt about him. Otherwise, I wouldn't feel right about being a part of his life.

I'd taken a long journey over the last year. It had started with me discovering what made me different and ended here, with me gaining control. A complete circle.

"He who is not courageous enough to take risks will accomplish nothing in life," Desi called.

Pulling my camera from my neck, I placed it in my camera bag and set it in the snow. "Wow. When did you become a philosopher?"

"I didn't," he replied. "But Muhammad Ali's words sure sounded good coming from me, right?"

I snorted. "I should have known."

Desi scooted closer, and then backed away again. "In all seriousness, Harper. Sometimes it takes risking yourself to realize yourself. And those *are* my words."

Risk. It was a four-letter word that held a big punch. Like *love* and *fear*. Actually, there were a lot of scary four-letter words. I made a list of them in my head: like, love, fear, lose, and fail.

Desi studied me. "The way I see it, the only way you're going to find out whether or not you can exist the way you want to in this world, despite your powers, is to fully put yourself out there. Why do you think things happened the way they did with Elias? You've held yourself back from feeling a full range of human emotions for so long that you intentionally separated your thoughts, turning them into an internal battle between the angel on one shoulder and the demon on the other. When really, your demon and angel are the same person."

It was more than I'd ever heard Desi say at one time. In that moment, I realized just how old and observant he really was.

My gaze returned to the shadows. "Come to me," I told them. They obeyed, lowering until they were eye level. "You belong to me. Not the other way around."

"We belong to each other," the shadows argued.

"I think you've gotten confused. You lived, you broke the rules, and you died to become a part of a terrible place full of terrible energy. You're not here to be redeemed. You're here to be controlled." My voice was confident. Most of the dark spirits who followed me had been people once, people who'd lived a life of crime and cruelty or who had sold their souls to darkness. In death, they had gone where all dark souls go.

It was the same for the lower-caste demons who also followed me. They were too weak where they came from to rise in rank, too weak to become the demons they really wanted to be.

I pitied them, but I wasn't their redemption. No matter how much they wanted me to be.

I'd drawn them in, my power a beacon of light. Which was ironic, since I brought darkness to the ones I loved the most.

My hand fell to my side, my fingers lifting the hem of my shirt to feel the skin beneath, to the raised scar that would always remind me of what had happened between me and the shadows. I'd been weak and injured then. I wasn't weak or injured now.

"We need boundaries, if this is going to work," I told them. "You either listen to me or I find a way to send you back to where you came from. Understood? Seriously, I'm the lesser of the evils here."

The spirits circled me, growing in density until they became a vortex of darkness. I was standing inside a funnel cloud, the center of a hurricane of hell.

They were testing me.

I thought back on my time in captivity, when I'd been trapped inside of a pitch-black room with nothing except the Collector's advice. Then, I'd been trying to escape the darkness and the shadows that liked to trail me.

"You were never meant to escape it. Embrace it," the Collector had said. *"Use them."*

I closed my eyes, then reopened them. The shadows were glowing, having transformed from the dark forms I was used to into black masses full of sparkling glitter. It was as if someone had poured jewels onto the night sky, and then turned the world upside down so that I was walking in space among the stars.

My mouth fell open, my eyes widening. This was the moment of truth.

I let myself be sad because my power fed off lesser-used emotions, tears spilling down my cheeks. My heart hurt, thoughts of Elias fresh, his love an open festering wound.

The frustration I felt, the ineptness, and the regret all gathered within me, and I fed off it, inhaling sharply.

The shadows were sucked toward me, as if they were liquid inside of a straw. Each time I inhaled, they drew closer until they were right in front of my face, a whisper on my lips before I swallowed them.

I felt like the wolf in *Little Red Riding Hood.*

When I was growing up, my aunt Eloise had either read me stories or played books on audio because I'd been unable to read. Since spirits came to me in words, and I'd once predicted a man's death by accident as a child through a written message, I hadn't been allowed to read or write. I'd been guarded and kept in check.

So much of my life had been regulated. All because I was innately evil.

Maybe this was why I'd related the most to the villains in fairy tales. The heroines had always been too perfect, their perfection part of what led to their victory. I'd felt sorry for the villains. Like the stepmother who'd been afraid of losing her beauty in *Snow White,* or the stepmother who'd been afraid of losing her position in *Cinderella.* They'd had real fears, real concerns. Things most of us fear, but are too afraid to admit. And they'd lashed out at the people they could have loved, had they faced their demons.

Fear. It's a mighty four-letter word.

The shadows' warmth pressed into my skin, chasing away the winter chill, as they seeped into my body through my pores, mouth, and nose.

I choked them down, my skin glowing, my vision sharpening. There was no doubt in my mind I looked like an ice queen at the moment, my skin luminous, my eyes chunks of coal.

Power filled me, and I reveled in it.

Control it, Harper, I told myself. *Don't let them control you.*

I was treading a fine line between giving in and taking over.

My skin hurt, and my heart pounded.

"*Harper,*" the shadows pleaded. "*Use us.*"

Greedy little bastards.

I may have related to the villains in the stories I'd heard growing up, but there was one way I differed.

I loved someone more than I loved power. I loved someone more than I feared failure. And I needed to show him I was worthy of him.

Love. It's a scary four-letter word. It's also a triumphant four-letter word.

"My way," I said. "This is going to be done my way."

The dark funnel cloud that had churned around me before now churned inside of me, growing in power, making my stomach hurt and my head throb.

I gritted my teeth. "My way!"

Swallowing hard, I focused on the ground before me, my hand reaching for the snow.

"Please," I whispered. Even though I felt confident, a little *please* to the universe couldn't hurt.

"Heat," I breathed. Energy rolled off me.

The snow melted before my eyes, turning the ice into slush around my boot-covered feet.

I laughed, and the shadows used the vulnerable moment to rocket out of me, desperate to escape.

"Holy wow!" Desi exclaimed.

My laughter continued, the sound relieved and gleeful all at once. All I'd done was melt a little snow, but it was a start. I'd controlled the shadows rather than letting them control me, even though it had hurt like hell.

Today, I had succeeded. Tomorrow, I might fail. But with each success I'd get stronger. With each failure, I'd learn something new.

This was the Harper I wanted and needed to be.

This was the Harper I was going to quit fighting. This was the Harper that was going to return to Elias.

~

For more than a week, I couldn't quit thinking about Elias and the way I felt around him.

Deep down, I knew the way we'd separated after making love had not been a bad thing. Even if it had been emotional and painful. I think, in retrospect, I'd gained strength from Elias, the kind of strength I needed to fight for myself on my own for the first time in my life. I'd needed this time to find a way to rein in my shadow demons enough that they wouldn't constantly torment him. That seriously wasn't healthy for a relationship.

Even so, I missed him so much it hurt. A week had passed, each day spent in different locations around Havenwood Falls while I practiced using the shadows. It helped me gain a confidence I'd been lacking, even though I failed as much as I succeeded.

The Court was watching me. I caught glimpses of Court members, their gazes tracking me, when I was around town, and I knew part of that was because of the striptease I'd done at Silk. There had been a lot of supernaturals present when I lost control, and the way I'd pulled magic from the Infernum had filled the space with a dark frenzy I knew people would talk about for weeks to come. The supernaturals, anyway.

The humans were, fortunately, completely oblivious.

For the first time in my life, I'd caused a true scandal. I kind of enjoyed being looked at in a different light. Even if it was embarrassing. The worst part was Aunt Eloise. Because she raised me, I thought of her more as my mother than my aunt, and she'd been giving me the side-eye ever since she overheard Irene Beckett telling one of the other busybodies in town that I had nice firm breasts. How Irene discovered things like that even when she wasn't present blew my mind.

Only Irene Beckett. The woman was incorrigible, her age and human status making her gossip all the more impressive. For some reason, the Court members respected her enough to leave her be, completely overlooking the fact that she knew too much about the supes when she wasn't a supe herself.

"Hmm," Aunt Eloise murmured when I entered her shop, her

head down, her lips pursed. It was a few days away from Valentine's Day, which was one of the busiest times of year for Eloise's Into the Mystic New Age shop. People got sentimental around Valentine's, especially those whose loved ones had passed on. Widows wanted to reconnect with their deceased spouses, and lovers wanted to talk with their deceased loves one final time.

I felt their anguish, and the angel I'd shared a bed with wasn't even dead. As a matter of fact, I was pretty sure he was close to impossible to kill.

"Would you quit *hmm*ing me already?" I requested, frowning. "So I did a thing, and it's over now."

The shop was a colorful mess of mismatched furniture, purple fabric, crystals, candles, books, and magical objects. As for where everything was located . . . well, that changed quite a bit. Aunt Eloise had a penchant for rearranging things. She also had an affinity for herbal teas and Van Morrison. As a matter of fact, she had a Morrison record playing on her turntable even now, the sound of it filling the space.

"Hmm," Aunt Eloise repeated, throwing me a look.

"What?" I asked.

"So it's over now?" she asked. "The whole stripping thing or Elias?"

My cheeks burned from embarrassment. "Elias isn't over. He's far from over."

Eloise sauntered toward me, as bright as ever in a pair of hot-pink leggings and a long-sleeved tunic covered in pink, puckered lips. Silver hoop earrings dangled from the bottom holes in her ears, a line of heart earrings fastened in the holes above them. Her white-streaked auburn hair was pulled up into a ponytail, held back by two pink scrunchies.

My aunt had always been this way, as loud in the way she dressed and looked as she was kind and compassionate in nature.

"So"—she leaned on the store's counter and placed her chin in her hands—"so what you're saying is that you—"

"Love him," I finished. It was easier to say out loud than I thought it would be, the words feeling warm and beautiful on my tongue.

Van Morrison crooned "Someone Like You" in the background, and Eloise sighed. "To be young again." Her gaze met mine. "Have you told him?"

I shook my head.

She glared. "Does he read minds, Harper? Because the last time I checked, angels had a hard time reading your thoughts because of the Infernum. Which means he needs to hear you say it."

"I needed to get control of something first," I said quietly.

There were things Aunt Eloise didn't know. Or maybe she did, and she pretended not to for my privacy's sake. She was a psychic, after all, which meant she could sense the darkness that followed me. Either way, I'd never spoken aloud to her about the shadows. Only those closest to me and the Court members actually knew about the spirits that trailed me. Eloise had kept her distance when the Court questioned me after the incident with the Collector. I hadn't wanted to burden her with my fears. She'd done enough raising me.

"And now?" Eloise asked.

I'd been working on my powers for more than a week while Desi guarded me. While I'd had trouble and even slipped up a few times, I'd gotten better and better at pulling the spirits into me and using their energy. It no longer hurt to open myself up to them, and they no longer fought to control me. I had a long way to go, possibly many years ahead, but I had enough control over them to keep them from bothering the man I loved. Which meant I could move forward.

I think the shadows were afraid I'd send them back into the Infernum forever, but they were wrong. Then I'd be at a disadvantage. I may not be a bad person, but I liked being able to express myself more. I liked knowing that if the time came that I needed to protect myself, I had the power to do just that. I had the power to control a shadow army.

The shadows no longer crowded me; their inky forms wavered in the distance until I called them forward.

I liked the way they made me feel wicked without me actually being wicked. I wanted to save the wicked for the one person I knew I could share it with, the one man I knew could handle that side of me.

My kind of wicked was perfect for the bedroom.

Visions of me and Elias, our limbs tangled together, popped into my head, and I fisted my hand into my shirt.

Please let him accept the darkness in me, I thought. I knew he didn't mind the demonic side of me, but I also knew by the look I'd seen in his eyes that he worried about it. Even if he pretended he didn't.

Valentine's Day was coming, and I wanted to prove to him—and to myself—that I was capable of being the strong woman he needed in his life.

"Are you going to the Cupids and Cuties party at Whisper Falls Inn this year?" Eloise asked suddenly. "Because I think maybe you should."

I'd never attended before. A masked formal affair, Cupids and Cuties was an annual Havenwood Falls event held on Valentine's Day for guests eighteen and older, where attendees could supposedly find their true love. My aunt had been on my case to attend since my eighteenth birthday.

Honestly, there was no reason for me to go.

"I'll be there." My response surprised both of us, my wide gaze meeting my aunt's equally wide stare.

"You're going?" she asked. "Really?"

I started to shake my head, but the word "yes" escaped my lips in the gesture's place.

Eloise whistled. "Well, I'll be damned, Harper. I thought it would be harder to convince you."

"You said I should go," I defended.

My aunt straightened, stepping away from the counter she'd been leaning on to check her appointment book. "Just don't strip."

"Aunt Eloise!"

She shrugged. "What? Did you think I was going to avoid saying that out loud forever?" Her eyes fell to my chest. "Luckily you took after your mother's side of the family."

"Aunt Eloise!" I protested again.

She tapped her appointment book. "I don't suppose you feel up to talking with the Juniper widower, huh? Poor guy comes every year, and

I don't have the heart to inform him that his wife keeps saying 'That damn bastard nagged me enough in life. Tell him to give me a break in death while I have the chance.'"

A snort escaped me. "Now that's romance."

The sarcastic joke automatically left my lips, but my thoughts weren't on the Junipers. They were on Elias.

My heart needed him.

CHAPTER 13

ELIAS

The embossed invitation had arrived three days ago with no return address.

Cupids & Cuties
Valentine's Day, Twilight
Whisper Falls Inn

Black tie affair.

I'd laughed my ass off first. Then, after I'd sat on my couch, staring at Harper's words still covering my kitchen wall, it hit me. The invitation had to be from her. Who else would send one to me? No one, that's who. No one in their right mind would invite me to some fancy party where, per the invite, "Cupid's aim strikes at the heart—that's how you know it's true love."

What the hell kind of shit was this?

With great reluctance, I dressed in formal black and headed toward the town square and Whisper Falls Inn. I shuffled my way inside behind the long line of arrivals as Michaela Petran greeted us at the door. In her hand were two items, both of which I was forced to take. The first was a white face mask.

"Seriously?" I cocked a brow.

"Love goes beyond what we can see on the outside," Michaela explained. "Cupid's aim strikes at the heart—that's how you know it's true love."

"Okay, and what's the arrow for?" I asked with a resigned shrug, looking at the white arrow with gold trim.

This time Michaela smirked at my tone. Surely she'd dealt with her fair share of men arriving under duress tonight. "When their aim is true, they'll light up for you. Follow the arrow's tip to your special lover's lips."

"Follow the arrow's tip?" I looked at the people behind me and leaned in. "You know what I am, Michaela. Can you please explain exactly how these little paper arrows work?"

Her lips pursed. "And ruin the fun?"

My blank face told her exactly what I thought of her fun. This type of party wasn't my idea of a good time to begin with, but add my stress, and the fact that I hadn't spoken to or seen Harper in nearly three weeks, and I was about ready to tell Michaela where she could stick her arrow.

"The magic doesn't lie." She winked.

I shook my head in disbelief and followed the flow of guests toward the ballroom on the first floor. Everything about this event shouted at me to turn around and run. The possibility of seeing Harper kept me rooted in place. The room wasn't packed, but there was a good turnout. More than I would have thought, considering a private date and a nice meal out seemed like the better option for tonight. Never underestimate a person's desire to know if their one true love is truly their one true love.

I tied on the mask and skimmed the crowd, looking for long brown locks and bright green eyes. It was the faded hue of an angel she wore that I spotted first—a mark of protection—only it was no longer Lucas's blue. It was a pale red. *My* mark alerted others she was watched over by angels. To most, that was deterrent enough to stay clear. I wished the mark gave her angelic gifts, because then she'd have that to help her with her own powers, but it was only a warning for those who might try to harm her.

My heart rate accelerated as I watched her speaking with her aunt Eloise, who stood by her side. Even though masks covered half their faces, I could spot the Sinclair women anywhere. *Angelic perks.*

It took twenty seconds of watching Harper's backside in the slim red column dress she wore before I walked her way. Thoughts and phrases tumbled over themselves to be the first to be said.

"I'm sorry."

"I miss you."

"I think I'm in love with you."

Something that proved I knew her demons and accepted them, and whatever came with them. Words failed when she turned around and I found her green eyes staring back at me.

~

HARPER

The arrow in my hand lit up, and I just knew it was him. I didn't need an event or even the arrow itself to tell me whom I was in love with. I knew. Heart, body, and soul, I simply *knew.*

The moment I looked up to find Elias Jamison gazing down at me, I wanted to soothe away the worry I saw in his eyes. His lips were slightly parted, as if there were words he wanted to say trapped by indecision. I'd done that to him.

He was magnificent in a black suit and tie, his broad frame filling it out in a way most men couldn't. Even with the mask he had pulled over his face, I would have known it was him. Well, with the beard, it was also kind of obvious.

Elias had always been there for me, even when he'd had his doubts. It was time for me to be there for him. I wasn't the same Harper I'd been a year ago. I was stronger, more confident, and brave. In large part because of him.

"Thank God, you got my invitation," Aunt Eloise exclaimed from behind me.

I should have been surprised by her declaration, but I wasn't. I'd wondered why she'd pushed me to attend, even after hearing about my declaration of love for the fallen angel. I think that's why I accepted her push to come without a fight. Because, somehow, I knew my aunt would get Elias here.

Startled, Elias's gaze shot up and away from me, but I placed my free hand against his arm to draw his attention back to me. This wasn't his kind of event, but he'd come, and I knew it was because of me. This was *my* Elias, and I loved him more than words could say.

Raising my glowing arrow, I pointed it at him and nodded at the lit up arrow in his own hand. "I think this is where we're supposed to kiss."

"Harper—" he began.

I didn't give him the chance to speak. Lifting onto my toes, I planted my lips against his in a gentle kiss that didn't demand anything. It simply said words I didn't think I could say here inside a crowded room.

"Can we do this somewhere else?" I asked, pulling away just enough to glance up into his face.

Elias yanked the mask off, his gaze fierce. "If you leave here with me, Harper, so help me—"

"I'm yours," I whispered. The shadows that followed me appeared behind him, hovering, and I shooed them away. The darkness didn't control me. I controlled it. "I'm yours."

Elias saw what I did, an impressed glint lighting up his eyes as his hand dropped down to mine, his fingers entwining with mine before tugging me toward the entrance.

Michaela tried to stop us at the door. "But you just got here," she protested.

We kept moving forward, dropping the arrows into her hands as we passed by. Elias and I were both reclusive people. It was one of the things that had drawn us together. We were wounded souls with too many stories to tell. Especially him.

I didn't ask where he was taking us, and I didn't care. Honestly, I barely remembered getting into his truck or the ride to our destination.

It hardly even registered that we were at his house before we were suddenly through his front door.

We shed our clothes before we even made it to the bedroom, leaving a trail of fabric from his front door to the side of his bed.

The words I'd scrawled on his kitchen wall were a blur as we passed by, sending a jolt through my soul. He'd kept the message. Maybe as a reminder? I knew, for me, it was imprinted in my brain and on my heart as the moment I took charge of my life, all in the name of love.

With Elias, I wanted what we had together to be forever, no matter the obstacles. No matter the dangers.

"Harper."

Coming up behind me, Elias whispered my name into my ear, the feel of his breath sending shivers down my spine. His voice and the warm feel of his body sent wet heat pooling between my legs.

"Harper." He embraced me, his naked frame a wall of steel against my softer flesh. Elias did things to me and for me that no one else had ever been able to do. I was open with him in a way I never could be before. He made me want to spend every day just being with him, and every night sleeping next to him naked. I never slept naked. I slept so overdressed it would make other people uncomfortable. At times, it made *me* uncomfortable, but clothes—even sleep clothes—had always been like a shield to me, a fabric barrier against the world. So many things had changed. For the better.

Tonight, right now, there was no shield, no barrier between my skin and Elias's.

"What—?" I began.

"Shhh." He didn't let me speak, his hand coming up to cover my eyes. "Don't look," he said. "Don't speak. Don't think. Just feel."

I didn't question him. I simply let myself get lost in the sensation, in this beautiful moment when the one person I never suspected would end up my lover was here with me now. Warm. Hard. Safe. In love.

Rather than turn me around, he kept my back to him, my backside pressed into his hard erection while his hand dropped away from my face. I didn't reopen my eyes, leaving them closed, because in truth I liked trusting him like this.

His lips found the sensitive spot just below my ear, his tongue teasing my skin, the feel of his beard adding even more friction, increasing my need. His hand moved over and down my chest, his fingers circling my nipple, gently tugging on it before continuing his journey south. The moment he touched my wet folds, I arched, a cry escaping my lips.

"That's it. Come for me, Harper. Let go." His whispered breath sounded strained yet controlled, his fingers working their magic against my clit.

I lost all strength in my legs. He guided me toward the bed, and my knees sank into his mattress, his large frame bent over mine.

"Please," I begged him.

I'd never made love this way before. I'd lost my virginity at twenty-three, but because I'd only ever had sex with two people, my second time with Elias, my knowledge was limited.

"God, Harper," Elias swore, his fingers bringing me to the edge of oblivion as he entered me from behind, his hips pumping hard and fast.

His fingers applied just the right amount of pressure on my clit, and I came, my muscles clenching around his cock. I screamed his name as his hand left the dampness between my thighs to grip my hips, his thrusts coming quicker and quicker until he stiffened, my name joining his in the still bedroom.

"Shit," Elias breathed, his arm circling my waist to guide me farther onto the bed before rolling us to the side. He slipped out of me, but he didn't let go, his limbs tangling with mine as he embraced me. His chin found my shoulder, and I tugged at his beard.

My emotions were everywhere, the feelings inside me a churning mess.

"I love you." The words slipped out of me unchecked, and I was suddenly glad my back was to him, my gaze on the room's opposite wall.

Elias grew still, our panted breaths the only response to my confession, before his hand suddenly found my chin.

He turned my head gently, leaning up just enough he could look down into my face. "Say that again." The way he looked at me was beautiful, an almost desperate plea in his eyes.

A smile played on my lips. "I love you." The words came easy, the emotion behind them strong. "L-O-V-E. Love, four letters."

Elias grinned. "Last time I checked, I could spell."

"You sure about that? Cause I've got a new hobby. Remember that list of firsts I used to have?"

"Yeah."

"Well, now I'm collecting four-letter words."

Elias laughed, and then sobered. "Please, for the love of God, tell me fuck is one of them."

"I don't know. I think I forgot how to spell. Care to show me instead?"

Elias didn't need any further invitation. This time, he rolled me over, taking me more gently, his lips next to my ear when I came for him. On an exhale, he breathed, "I love you, Harper Sinclair."

I'd never felt so darkly seductive in my life, and yet so full of light and life.

Instead of finding his own release, Elias surprised me by slowing his thrusts, his body stroking mine with a deliberate laziness that extended my pleasure with little aftershocks.

"I think I have another four-letter word for you," he muttered as he teased my neck with his beard.

I clutched at his hip, unsure if I wanted him to stop or if I wanted to go again. "Yeah?"

Jerking his hips, he buried himself deeply. "Mine." He lifted his head and brushed my hair away from my face. "You're mine, Ms. Sinclair. You, Desi, and every one of your shadows—I accept you all."

Lifting my hips to draw him deeper, I touched his cheek. "And we accept you."

The angel born of light and the human born from darkness. The odds were against us, but with love and acceptance on our side we could overcome any obstacles.

EPILOGUE

ELIAS

y fingers traced a lazy path along Harper's inner thigh as she slept soundly beside me. Two months together, and I couldn't stop touching her. I doubted if I would ever get enough of her. She'd teased me again and again about watching her sleep.

"Why don't you watch a movie, or read a book, instead of lying here staring at me?" she'd ask. "Don't you get bored?"

Not a chance in hell. My new favorite pastime was studying her. I loved how her flesh faded from passion-tinted pink after we made love to its normal creamy tone. How she slept curled into her side with her hand shoved under her cheek, as she was right now. I spent many nights studying her facial expressions, always watching for that change that told me her shadows were taking hold. I never tried to wake her from her demon-possessed sleepwalking. But I did keep a notepad and pen on nearly every surface of my place and hers. No more writing on the walls for my little *umbra amans*.

I was deeply in love with this woman. Inching closer, I kissed her shoulder gently. In Harper I had found the purpose I'd lost when I'd come to earth.

My hand moved closer to the heat between Harper's thighs, and she sighed, her bare ass shifting backward to grind against me. "This is why I tell you to watch movies."

I chuckled at her sleepy, disgruntled tone. "Am I bothering you?" I teased, my middle finger skimming close enough to know her body was more than ready for me.

"Not in the least." She arched her back and turned, looking over her shoulder.

I cupped her sex and leaned forward to meet her kiss when a ripping pain tore down my spine.

"What the—" I lurched to my knees with a gasp.

"Elias?" Harper's voice shook, panic making it sharp.

"I'm okay. I—" A brilliant light filled my vision, blinding me, as my back erupted with white-hot burning. "Shit."

Harper screamed.

"Harper?" I reached out, searching for her hand.

"I'm right here." Her shaking fingers clutched mine. "What's happening?" Her voice joined the chattering coming from her shadows.

As though my back was tied to bungee cords, twin joints punched through my shoulder blades and threw me off balance, sending me into Harper.

I righted myself, my hands gripping at her arms as my vision cleared. "Are you all right?"

Harper nodded, her green eyes wide. "You . . . um, you've got . . ." Her trembling hand waved toward something over my shoulder.

Black shadows fluttered in my peripheral vision. I twisted around, expecting to see Harper's demons lingering, and was met with inky black and blue feathers. My stomach dropped, and I leapt from our bed.

Wings. Heat rushed through me as my emotions went crazy. *I have wings.*

My gaze went skyward. "Is this a joke?"

Rolling my shoulders, I pulled the limbs forward, wrapping them around my body. I'd lost my wings a century ago. The silky touch of feathers against my skin stole the air from my lungs. *Why?*

"Elias?" Harper whispered. Parting the curtain of my wings, I thrust my hand out and pulled her into my arms. I hid my face in the crook of her neck and shoulder, holding her naked body to mine. "You have wings. They're amazing."

Why the hell do I have wings? Leaning back, I brushed a tear from Harper's cheek. I stretched my newly acquired wings to their full span. It was like they'd never been torn from my body. The feathers twitched, as though they'd heard my thoughts. Our bond had already formed. "What is this?"

The telltale scrape of Desi's barbs screeched across the floor, and I knew by the way he entered the space that he knew something.

"This is fate, angel," Desi said as he stopped in the middle of the bedroom. Harper and I shared a glance. Fate. Another four-letter word. The sentient weapon paused before adding, "You will need every advantage you can get for what's to come. You must protect her. You must protect this town."

Harper stiffened in my arms, her eyes fixed on Desi. "How do you know?"

With a knowing sigh, I laced my fingers with Harper's. "The Destroyer would know. His connections run deep."

My wings were back because I was a Dominion angel who'd just been granted a guardianship.

We hope you enjoyed this story in the Havenwood Falls world featuring a variety of supernatural creatures. If you want to read more about Harper, her story begins with *Ink & Fire* by R.K. Ryals and continues with *The Collector: Awakening*, both in the main Havenwood Falls series. You can also see more of Elias in *Awaken the Soul* and *Avenge the Heart* both by Michele G. Miller, in the Havenwood Falls High series.

Havenwood Falls is a collaborative effort by multiple authors.

Books in the Havenwood Falls Sin & Silk series:

Taming the Beast by Nadirah Foxx
Plans Laid Bare by JD Nelson
Shift of Fate by Victoria Escobar
Stolen Wishes by Victoria Flynn
Damned Allure by Justine Winter
Savage Salvation by Kristie Cook
Dark Seduction by Michele G. Miller & R.K. Ryals
Soul Laid Bare by JD Nelson
Stray With Me by E.J. Fechenda
Chase the Flames by Desiree Lafawn
Flirting With Death by Nadirah Foxx

Also try the signature line, Havenwood Falls, and the historical paranormal line, Legends of Havenwood Falls.

Stay up to date at www.HavenwoodFalls.com

Subscribe to our reader group and receive free stories and more!

ABOUT THE AUTHOR

Writing-obsessed since childhood, Michele once failed seventh-grade math in pursuit of the perfect teen drama (anything for her craft!). These days she fails at housework, cooking, and getting to the school pickup line on time in pursuit of the perfect plot.

Michele writes novels with fairytale love for everyday life. Romance is central to her plots where the genres range from Coming of Age Fantasy and Realistic Fiction to New Adult Romantic Suspense. Among other titles, she is the author of the bestselling From the Wreckage series, a Havenwood Falls author, and co-writes the Paper Planes series with author Mindy Hayes. Mindy and Michele also write clean contemporary titles under the pen name Mindy Michele.

Michele is represented by Italia Gandolfo of Gandolfo Helin & Fountain Literary Management.

Spoiler Alert: Michele still fails at math.

Website: http://www.michelegmillerbooks.com/
Facebook: https://www.facebook.com/AuthorMicheleGMiller
Twitter: https://twitter.com/chelemybelles
Pinterest: http://pinterest.com/chelemybelles/
Instagram: https://instagram.com/chelemybelles/

ABOUT THE AUTHOR

R.K. Ryals is the author of emotional and gripping young adult and new adult paranormal romance, contemporary romance, and fantasy. With a strong passion for charity and literacy, she works as a full-time writer encouraging people to "share the love of reading one book at a time." An avid animal lover and self-proclaimed coffee-holic, R.K. Ryals was born in Jackson, Mississippi, and makes her home in the Southern U.S. with her husband, her three daughters, two playful cats named Delphi and Paris, and a coffeepot she honestly couldn't live without. Should she ever become the owner of a fire-breathing dragon (tame of course), her life would be complete. Visit her at www.authorrkryals.com.

ACKNOWLEDGMENTS

Michele:

"I'm so grateful to the people who support me through the book process and life:

My husband and kids deal with me forgetting laundry, dinner, carpool, emails, and the list goes on. How they put up with me I'll never know!

My amazing crew of readers, bloggers, and friends—on Facebook and in real life— keep me sane. You make this solitary writer life a little less solitary, and a lot more lifelike.

My core reader groups on Facebook, Chele's Belles and Mindy and Michele's M&M's: Thanks for being a sounding board when needed, book pimps when needed, and friends always.

To Jo Pettibone: Thank you for walking with me from day one with Viv, Breck, and Elias. And for being the best alpha a writer could have. I'm so lucky to have you. Oh! And for the cookies and brownies you send me. When's the next shipment? (wink)

To the Havenwood Falls family: This group continues to grow, but their generosity, creativity, and enthusiasm for this project astounds me. I'm so lucky to be able to write and collaborate with these amazing creatives. Many of the characters and places I mention in my Havenwood Falls books were created by others in this amazing group.

More specifically, thanks to these ladies for creating and sharing your characters with us in *Dark Seduction*: Randi Cooley Wilson and Kristie Cook. Liz Ferry for your editing genius, and Regina Wamba for your kick-butt cover design.

I can't forget a shout-out to R.K. Ryals for agreeing to co-write #Harlias with me. You have been a dream to work with, my friend.

And of course, a final HUGE thank you to Kristie Cook for creating Havenwood Falls and making this all possible. I will forever be in awe of your business savvy and ingenuity. I'm honored to be a part of this world and blessed to have you as a friend.

R. K.:

I am so thankful to be a part of the Havenwood Falls journey. Writing this story was an adventure I will never forget.

This story would not have been possible without our fearless leader, Kristie Cook. Thank you so much for creating a town that brings authors and characters together in a unique and amazing way. I am so grateful that you are a part of my life.

I am always blown away by the amount of people it takes to bring a story together. There are so many that I want to thank.

First, I have to thank my husband, whose patience and diligence is always such a support for me. To my daughters, who inspire me on a daily basis. I am truly blessed with amazing children. They have passion, determination, and resilience. Raising them to be the strong women I am watching them become humbles me.

A heartfelt thank you to my personal assistant, Christina Silcox. Not only does Christina assist me so much in life, she is a beacon of strength. I am amazed by everything she does.

To Melissa Wright, Jessica Johnson, and Amanda Engelkes, who are always letting me use them for a sounding board. Your input and your suggestions always mean so much to me.

A special thank you to a group of loyal women who have followed me since the beginning of my career. To my Archive girls and my Scribes group. The dedication you have shown me is not taken for granted.

There are no words big enough to express how grateful I am to be a part of the Havenwood Falls family. Huge thanks and crushing hugs to the Havenwood Falls authors who let me borrow the wonderful characters that make this story so strong. To the rest of the

Havenwood Falls authors for the characters they've created. This town is possible because of all of you.

A massive shout out to Regina Wamba for the beautiful cover art. You are seriously incredible.

To Liz Ferry and Kristie Cook for your amazing editing. You make these books so much stronger.

A very special thank you to my co-author, Michele G. Miller, for being such an amazing writing partner.

Finally, to my readers, you take my breath away. It means the world that you read my words. I am extremely grateful for your support on this insane journey full of crazy twists and turns. My love to you always.

AN EXCERPT

Soul Laid Bare (A Havenwood Falls Sin & Silk Novella) by J.D. Nelson

The story of Mavis and Cameron's romance and fight to be together continues in this sequel to *Plans Laid Bare*.

With the fear of discovery by her evil grandfather behind her and her demonic power growing stronger every day, Mavis LeGrand is content in the mountains of Colorado. Her incubus fiancé, Cameron, loves her, and things seem to be going as well as can be expected, but she knows behind the picturesque town and smiling faces, an evil lurks, just waiting for her to let her guard down long enough to snatch away the peace she's found.

Determined to push through her growing unease, Mavis throws herself into finding a way to get Cameron's soul back from her soon-to-be father-in-law. At the same time, she's dealing with the incubus's insatiable desires and the budding romance between her best friend and the ridiculously unsuitable demon who's crashing in their spare bedroom.

With a strong feeling of malice lingering over the town like a dense fog, Mavis can sense that she'll soon be in for a fight, albeit a battle she knows she can win. Evil has no place in Havenwood Falls, and she'll be damned if she lets anyone or anything hurt the town or the ones she loves.

SOUL LAID BARE

BY J.D. NELSON

As I filled out my billionth online job application for the month, I lamented the fact that I couldn't add *demon-killing badass* to my list of job skills. I mean, what's the use of having a kick-ass power like that if you couldn't use it to pad a skimpy résumé? Sure, accounting had fascinated me in my pre–Exitium Daemonium days, but now, it bored me to tears. These days, I needed a job that had a bit of excitement and room to be promoted, not a dull stay-at-home position where my best coworker friend was a calculator.

"Ugh," I said, sighing as I stood up from Cameron's desk and stretched. "I'm officially sick of the job hunt. I think I'm going to take a page out of your book and become an escort."

"What was that, darling?" asked a deep voice gruff with sleep.

"Nothing," I told my fiancé, ogling his muscled chest and the erection lifting the sheet as I climbed onto our king-sized bed to join him. "Well, nothing unless you like dull employment that makes you want to tear your hair out by the roots."

He flashed the devilish grin he knew made me weak in the knees and stroked my hair back from my forehead. "How could I like anything that changes one strand of your beautiful blond hair?"

"So," I said, straddling his hips and leaning in for a kiss. "You think my hair is beautiful?"

Cameron tugged me tight against his erection, a smoldering look of desire in his honey-brown eyes. "I think every part of you is beautiful, Mavis, no matter what color your hair."

I closed my eyes and let my body gradually change from a blond-haired, blue-eyed young woman to the pale demon with white-blond hair and silver eyes he preferred. "Better?"

He grinned and lifted my shirt over my head, taking care not to catch it on the tiny twin horns above my hairline. "As soon as I get you naked, it will be."

"I think I can make that happen," I told him, giggling as he shivered from the chill of my partially ice-covered skin.

A loud bang sounded against the wall we shared with our neighbor, making us both jump. Cam groaned and glared at the wall. "For the love of everything holy."

I suppressed another giggle. "I guess Penelope is awake . . . and still in her sex drought."

"I'm willing to ignore her if you are," he said, thumbing my hardened nipples through my bra.

I rocked against him, lost in the sensation, and gasped out, "You know she won't stop," when he fell into rhythm with me.

He sighed and flopped back onto his pillow, giving up. "Fine, but if she doesn't let us have some very enthusiastic sex in my own bed soon, we're moving to Tibet."

I laughed at his cynicism, but on this one, I was in perfect agreement with him. She had interrupted us so many times in the last week, I was thinking about talking to the management about permanent soundproofing or maybe even eviction.

But to be entirely fair, our mutual bestie wasn't exactly keeping us completely celibate. Because of Cam's nearly insatiable incubus appetite, we were still having sex two or three times a day. We just weren't allowed to have sex within earshot of our not-by-choice-chaste neighbor.

To be honest, I didn't care where we had it as long as we had it. Cam's father might have taken his humanity when he'd taken his soul, but he was still the same tall, dark, and inappropriate guy I'd met on the side of the road five months ago while I was on the run from my own crazed family member. In almost every single way, he hadn't changed one bit. He still made me laugh with his charming, sarcastic wit, and, of course, he was still the sexed-up asshole I wanted to smack upside the back of his head on occasion.

All in all, I couldn't complain too much. Things were pretty close to perfect in the little life we'd carved out in Havenwood Falls—apart from Cam's stolen soul; the looming threat of my future father-in-law, Severin DeSalle, trying to kidnap me to use my demon-killing power for his own evil purposes; my jobless state; and a neighbor actively trying to keep me from getting laid, that is.

Okay, so maybe things weren't that great. But we had to play the hand we were dealt, right?

Penelope knocked on my front door mere seconds after she heard Cam reluctantly leave to meet his latest client. Brunette and bubbly, the brown-eyed beauty usually had a happy expression pasted on her face, but what stood in front of me on this day was a downtrodden, hopeless wreck.

"What's wrong?" I asked, pulling her inside to keep the heat from escaping. Ice demon or not, I wasn't immune to Colorado's frigid temperatures, and Penelope was an expert at complaining about my cold apartment . . . or really anything that was pissing her off.

"It's Ray," she said, sighing as she shed her bright red coat.

"Nooooo," I whined. "No more demon problems, Penny. I have enough demon problems of my own, you know."

She frowned. "That six-month deadline Severin implemented is coming up pretty quickly, isn't it?"

"Very," I muttered, taking the coat from her and hanging it on a hook near the door. "But it's not as if I'm actually going to let him use me or my powers for his plot for world domination or whatever he's up to."

Brows raised, she asked, "Oh, have you and Cam finally come up with a plan to stop him?"

"No. Well, sort of. Do you think sticking my size sixes up his ass will work?"

"I don't know," she said, smirking. "He's an incubus. He might actually like that."

I glared at her. "I'm telling Cam you said that."

She glared back. "Fine."

"And then I'm telling Ray you want to have his demon baby," I added for good measure.

Penelope looked off into the distance and shrugged.

"Penny, no."

She threw her hands up, exasperated. "Well, what do you expect? The constant innuendo is slowly wearing me down. Realistically, I don't know how much longer I can resist him."

My jaw dropped. "He's actually wearing you down with those terrible sex jokes and thinly veiled come-ons?" I shook my head. "You know, I think that might say more about you than him."

"Yes! And screw you!" she exclaimed, throwing herself into the corner chair. "Do you know how hard it is to turn down sex from a hot demon like Ray?"

I stared at her. "Are you seriously asking me that question right now?"

She laughed, remembering her interference in my super-sexy-happy-fun-time this morning. "Oh, yeah. I guess you do."

"Of course I do! You won't let me have mind-blowing sex with my freakin' fiancé in my own bed, you jealous cow!"

Penelope threw her hands up. "Do you think I want to stop you?"

I raised an eyebrow.

"Okay, maybe I do, but fuck, Mavis, I can't take hearing the constant banging anymore. I'm about to start humping the furniture over there!"

I wrinkled my nose. "Gross. Stay away from the couch. We just managed to get that spot of disintegrated evil henchman out of it."

"Ew."

"No more 'ew' than you lusting after Rayonus," I said.

"He's Ray," she deadpanned.

She had a point there. Rayonus Rixa, or Ray as we called him in secret, was smoking hot. He was tall and dark-haired with a creepy bright blue and solid black eye combo that would give any normal woman nightmares, but he was also every bit the devious, troublemaking demon your mother warned you about. He had a knack for always being there with a bad idea or to influence you into doing something you'd normally never do. For Penelope, he was her sexual kryptonite. For me, he was a good demon friend of Cam's that had been squatting in our guest bedroom for the past four months.

Penelope sighed. "I don't know how much more sexual tension I can take before I crack, Mavis. Every time he stares me down with that black demon eye of his, I need a fresh pair of panties. Why is that so fucking hot?"

"What's this about needing new panties?" Ray asked, opening the front door and stomping the snow off his boots.

"You could knock, you know," I griped.

A smile spread across his disturbingly handsome face as he said, "I could, indeed, Miss LeGrand, but then I wouldn't hear half of the dirty things that come out of Penny's mouth." Then he hung his coat next to Penelope's and traipsed into the kitchen like he didn't have a care in the world.

I rolled my eyes. If anything, Ray was consistent with the effortless charm and bullshit.

When he was out of hearing distance, I sat on the arm of Penelope's chair and leaned over to ask, "Have you considered just getting it over with? It's clear both of you want to fuck each other's brains out."

"He's a demon," she said, as if that settled it.

"Um, I'm a demon," I countered.

"Yeah, but you're a good demon, and you're not trying to fuck me."

"True, but you don't know that Ray isn't decent deep, deep, deep down."

She lifted an eyebrow. "I don't?"

"Okay, he's probably not," I conceded. "But a little demon dick won't kill you, Penelope. Ray can't take your soul like Cam can."

"I don't need a little demon dick!" Penelope hissed.

"That's good to hear," Ray said, coming out of the kitchen with a glass of water. "Because I've got more than you can handle, Penny."

"Stop calling me Penny!" she snapped at him.

He inclined his head, a small smile playing on his lips. "As you wish, Miss Osbourne."

Penelope and I rolled our eyes and went back to ignoring him.

"I was thinking about going to Callie's," I said, changing the subject. "Do you want to tag along after work tomorrow? I remember you saying you needed a skirt to go with that white eyelet top."

Before Penelope could answer, Ray said, "A skirt is a fantastic idea, Penny. I do love easy access."

"Don't you have somewhere to be?" I asked, annoyed. "And before you answer, remember that I can destroy you where you stand."

The sarcastic smile he wore fell from his lips. "You know, I do think I have an appointment elsewhere. I believe I'll bid you beautiful ladies adieu for the afternoon."

Penelope watched him quickly retreat with a wistful expression. "He's going to my apartment, isn't he?"

"You're the one who showed him where you keep the spare key," I pointed out, shaking my head. "Honestly, I don't know why you're putting off the inevitable. Fuck him or don't fuck him—I don't care—but you have to do something soon. This can't go on forever. Cameron is starting to get really pissed with the blue-ball situation you're forcing on him."

She groaned and buried her face in a beaded throw pillow. "I'm doomed."

"Doomed is better than damned around here these days," I reminded her, shrugging.

She lifted her head and narrowed her eyes at me. "I think Cam and Ray are starting to be a really shitty influence on you."

Purchase *Soul Laid Bare* where books are sold.